GODDAMN THIS WAR!

GODDAMN THIS WAR!

Art & story by
TARDI

Chronology by
JEAN-PIERRE VERNEY

Translated by **Helge Dascher** | Edited by **Kim Thompson** | Series design by **Adam Grano** | Production by **Paul Baresh and Emory Liu** | Font designed by **Allan Haverholm,** provided by **Christopher Ouzman** of **Faraos Cigarer** | Associate Publisher **Eric Reynolds** | Published by **Gary Groth** and **Kim Thompson** | Translation assistance by **John Kadlecek** | Editorial assistance by **Janice Lee** | *Goddamn This War!* (*Putain de Guerre!*) © 2013 **Editions Casterman** | This edition © 2013 **Fantagraphics Books** | All rights reserved, permission to quote or reproduce material for reviews or notices must be obtained from **Fantagraphics Books**, in writing, at **7563 Lake City Way NE, Seattle, WA 98115** | Visit the Fantagraphics website at **www.fantagraphics.com** | First edition: **April, 2013** | Printed in Singapore | ISBN: **978-1-60699-582-2.**

1914

"Mobilization is not war. Under the present circumstances, it appears on the contrary to be the best means of assuring peace with honor."
Raymond POINCARÉ, President of the Republic, August 2, 1914.

"I consider these events to be most fortunate—indeed, I have been awaiting them for forty years. France is remaking herself, and in my opinion, she could not do so without a purifying war."
Alfred BAUDRILLARD, Bishop, *Le Matin,* August 16, 1914.

There we were, under the scorching sun: France's little soldiers, trampling through fields of wheat, fields of glory on our minds, with a knot of fear in our guts and a load of shit in our pants.

We were utterly cocksure, though. The moment we left Paris, we'd already taken Berlin in our minds. This was our shot at getting even for 1870, now that those pain-in-the-ass Huns were at it again.

But this time we were ready. We were gonna stuff their boiled leather helmets down their throats, spikes and all.

The kids loved seeing us heroes troop on by, with the marching band out front. It was a piss-poor example to be setting, but they'd been so brainwashed at school and in church they would've followed us to the slaughter if we'd let them.

The experts in the General Staff had assured us: Germany would respect Belgium's neutrality. ...And then the Germans invaded brave, neutral little Belgium. The civilians were fleeing the war, and I would've cheerfully joined them.

Naturally, the Prussians were staying in the civilians' homes, eating their jam, sleeping in their flea-ridden beds, and guzzling their well water. But while the locals streamed out, we streamed in, as if drawn to trouble.

It was really something, all the expensive equipment we were demolishing, considering I knew people who didn't own a pot to cook in!

We finally got to see some Germans, being led out of destroyed villages in forced marches. It was our first chance to examine the enemy. They didn't look like bad guys... In fact, they looked like us.

They were prisoners, and I would've given a lot to be in their shoes. Their war was over.

As dawn was breaking, we came across some dragoons who were observing the German advances. They had a vegetable cart with them, outfitted with a lethal little automatic for stopping the Krauts in their tracks. We didn't doubt for a second that they'd succeed.

People should've considered the inevitable hardships ahead of time. I mean, I'd thought of them, and it's not as if I was any smarter than anyone else. But what could I have done? How could one person have warned the world? Would I have been allowed to speak out? Would anyone have listened to a lathe operator from Rue des Panoyaux? Hardly.

This was the moment when the 20th century really began, in all its viciousness and bloody-mindedness. Me, I had imagination in spades, though. I saw myself as a corpse, swept into this stream of fools against my will, along with thousands, millions of other corpses, and I didn't like it one little bit.

The other guys, still waiting on the platform at the Gare de l'Est, already saw themselves throwing back a well-earned beer on the Alexanderplatz.

Only the mothers really knew. They knew the babies in their arms were tomorrow's war orphans, and the cattle cars (8 horses, 40 men) were nothing but rail-mounted coffins joined end to end and headed for military cemeteries.

According to the Kaiser, the Germans were "missionaries of human progress," "chosen by God to civilize the world." But they couldn't see beyond their rifle sights either... Well, a few of them could, but of course they were ignored.

Viennese ballroom dancers, sons of good families, cultivated aristocrats and poets – all of them had their sabers ready, eager to chop off the breasts of Serbian women to avenge the Archduke's assassination. The game of alliances was on, running like well-tuned machinery. Those early days of August saw Europe rush headlong into horror.

The kindly Berlin baker was seeing himself on the Champs-Élysées, dunking a pastry into a café au lait and admiring Paris' little ladies, so pretty and so fresh... Talk about imagination!

So much human meat was needed to satisfy the insatiable appetites of Europe's masters.

And so much animal meat to feed the men who would soon die, their guts still stuffed with the warm, pungent flesh of those beasts.

The need was endless, since we were all marked for slaughter.

We didn't need a map or compass to figure out after a while that we weren't headed in the right direction any more. "It's 1870 all over again," said the old-timers. We were pulling back.

I felt very alone. I shouldn't've strayed from the pack, but that's how I was. I just wasn't keen on collective sacrifice.

It's no fun, having to move around without any cover. A single bullet from the muzzle of a nasty Mauser operated by some fucking fastidious little Kraut could leave you in the hay for good. One second you're shaking like a leaf, the next you're a worthless corpse.

I wasn't keen on pointless stupidity either, and in this sun-drenched slaughter-house, the idea of going home was looking better by the minute.

I'd make a perfect fatality if I just vanished in the confusion. An anonymous heap of decaying flesh, a missing person. Who would worry about a lathe worker employed by the Biscorne Factory, living on Rue des Panoyaux, in the 20th arrondissement of Paris? When the poor die, nobody gives a shit.

The day'd been hot and deadly. And then, as if that wasn't enough, we were advised of the presence of Prussian soldiers in the thicket below our pasture.

We could barely make them out. Their position was a lot better than ours.

There was no way to stop what was happening. Someone should've said: "This is going to end badly!" But there was no time to chat. It was too late. It was too much to ask — we couldn't think any more.

We looked like a walking flea market, what with our mess tins and all the crap we had to lug. Add to that the clatter of our pots, pans and shovels, and you could say we didn't exactly blend into the landscape, especially in our circus outfits. We were ideal targets out there.

So it wasn't real smart on our little lieutenant's part to stick us right in the middle of the fucking meadow, our gear poking above the alfalfa, with nothing but dandelion stems to shield us from the bullets the Boches were about to lodge in our guts.

I was feeling like shit as that moronic assault got underway. I tucked my head between my shoulders and clutched the butt of my rifle against my belly.

The little lieutenant didn't last long, screwing around in the front row like that. To this day, I wonder whether we should've followed him at all.

Positioned at the back end of their magnificent little 75s, the artillery were busy killing, drunk with the smell of gunpowder and the song of their guns. Maybe they got their peace of mind from the few miles that separated them from the bodies torn apart by their shells. Who knows?

And then it was quiet again. ...Except for the screams of the dying. During the attack, under a hail of shells, I'd let myself fall behind so I could play dead in the woods. I still had the shakes when I noticed a Boche snoozing on my shoulder.

Had he pulled the same stunt as me? Was he just out to save his skin, and fuck all this slaughter that didn't concern him? The possibility made him seem like he might be a decent guy, but I didn't know for sure.

And then a spiked helmet stumbled by, without seeing us. I didn't have to wait long to find out what he was doing here, away from the others.

He'd come to take a shit on the sacred soil of France, the "eldest daughter of the Church."

Did he void all his fear out of his guts? Either way, the filthy bugger never got around to wiping his ass.

The dragoons ran him right through. Some relief, huh? Goodbye war... Goodbye to the country holiday, the little outings on the banks of the Marne, the open-air cafés, the boating party.

That was the last I of saw of Spikey's pink hindquarters. I left my Boche to his dreams of conquest and cleared the hell out.

The dragoons, with their horsehair tails and thick whips, caught up with a couple of comrades. Their exhausted steeds already smelled like carrion.

Several lancers charged, hell-bent on skewering them. I've always been terrified of horses. Give me a bike any day.

You couldn't tell if it was German Krupp or French Schneider shells raining down. Either way, the artillery was doing a bang-up job.

So much for the heroic charge! Hardly a horse or man came back happy from that little pastoral outing.

On reflection, I figured the horses were partly to blame for the awful mess. After all, they'd agreed to carry these lethal creatures on their backs... I think maybe I was starting to lose it.

There were no taxi rides to the front for the zouaves, those "indigenous" foot soldiers we didn't yet have the balls to call Moroccans. One of them pointed me in the direction of my regiment.

I slipped back into the herd unnoticed. It looked like the Germans were retreating. So of course we needed to hurry on up and dog their heels.

In the field, there were amateurs like us, and then there were pros like the Limeys, who laughed their asses off at our ancient gear and bright red pants. Our sideshow outfits really did stand out. They were a bit dated, but great for target practice.

The Belgians were floundering. They'd opened the sluice gates to flood the invaders, and now the "Jass" and their king were ankle-deep in water as they clung to their last small shred of territory, while the Boche goose-stepped across Brussels' main square.

Fall came. The cannons grew quieter as munitions supplies ran short on both sides — they had a shot to call the whole thing off and they blew it. We built funeral pyres and, while the unidentified dead went up in smoke, we began to stake out our positions. The Germans had fallen back only to dig in more deeply. It was clear that they still planned on coming back to teach us how to make sauerkraut.

The Tommies weren't unhappy about the move. It was their "God and my lawful right" against the Germans' "God with us." There was no way that was going to end well. And who was this God? Another hypo-crite with a finger in every pie.

"Each for himself and God against all": now that's the slogan every kid ought to know.

Meanwhile, the big question troubling us Frogs, of course, was whether the Scots, who walked so bravely to their deaths, wore skiwies or if their balls were swinging loose beneath their kilts.

I'd just taken part in the Battle of the Marne. I hadn't really understood what was going on, but then again, nothing had been explained to me. So I didn't realize that I'd just entered into the French history books as a hero, and that I was deeper in shit than ever.

We dug our first trenches. Gone were the days of the little toy soldiers, in rows of four, eight or sixteen. We'd turned into ditch diggers, conscientiously digging our own mass graves.

Once we climbed down into our tombs, we understood that we'd be there for a while. The Boches weren't heading home anytime soon, and Berlin was still far away. At Christmas, a truce gave way to fraternization, mostly between the Brits and the Krauts. Good will was in the air. We spent a couple hours trading cigarettes and candy, and then we went back to our dugouts to start killing each other again.

One thing I knew for sure was that we were settling in for a long war.

1915

"The best way to defeat one's enemies is, first, to kill them.
It's worth pointing out such basic truths, which are so obvious today,
while the impressions are still vivid. It will be too late after the victory."
General Pierre-Joseph-Maine CHERFILS, *L'Écho de Paris*, April 1915

"One of the surprises of this war and one of its marvels remains the extraordinary role poetry has played."
Paul BOURGET, *L'Écho de Paris*, June 20, 1915

The big guns were spitting shells from behind the lines. Our artillery-men were having a field day at the ass end of their old fortress hardware. Since we were short on heavy artillery, we'd stripped the forts and hauled out the antiques so we could pound the Huns, hoping they'd stay nice and quiet down in their holes.

The Germans made a point of returning the favor, with precision and deter-mination. Every time a German coal box landed on our heads, Morille, the squad corporal, would say, "Here comes the mail!" What a card, that Morille. They broke the mold after that one...

Looking like armed panhandlers, we reinforced our dugouts whenever there was a lull. We froze our asses off at the loopholes, eyes glued to the other side, our guts clenched in fear and our noses running.

The guns barked at the same time every day. The Germans would reply. Sometimes, without warning, they'd initiate the carnage. Men would be turned into mangled masses of flesh, mud, broken bones, spilled guts, dismembered parts, human debris you couldn't look at.,. The horror! The horror! The horror!

I'd have liked to see all the wise guys right there, in the heart of the inferno: Joffre, the president, the Kaiser, the ministers, the priests and every last general. And my mother, too, for bringing me into this world.

The Germans, who enjoyed working with wood, had laid out their trenches meticulously. We could tell from their setup that they were planning to stay for a while, committed as ever to smashing our defenses and forcing us to hand over our afternoon tea. But they weren't in a celebrating mood either.

They didn't seem to get tired of pounding away at us. Their weapons were better than ours. They took pride in their highly efficient war industry and, needless to say, we bore the brunt of it.

We responded in kind, of course, caught up in a savage frenzy fueled by forty years of sanctioned hatred on both sides. A monster had emerged, and its pestilential breath billowed from the cannons' mouths.

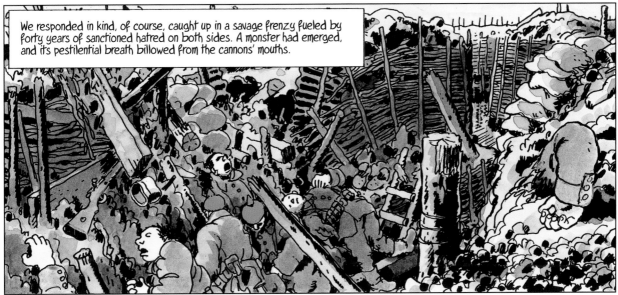

Do you have any idea how we felt, starting another goddamn day out on the front line, after yet another night at the bottom of a cold, damp dugout, sprawled out on straw that was turning to slime beneath us, with rats and lice all around, and the ripe stench of farts, feet, and the corpses decaying outside?

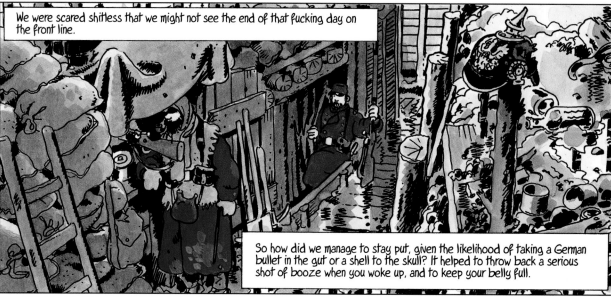

We were scared shitless that we might not see the end of that fucking day on the front line.

So how did we manage to stay put, given the likelihood of taking a German bullet in the gut or a shell to the skull? It helped to throw back a serious shot of booze when you woke up, and to keep your belly full.

What we should've done is clear out and leave nothing behind but our guns. Except we had the cops at our backs, and we could still remember the carcasses of the exhausted stragglers they'd gunned down during the retreat. Like they say, we were between a rock and a hard place. A German bullet or the post. "Desertion in the face of the enemy" got you twelve French bullets to the heart.

We didn't have a lot of options in our role as future "Soldiers Who Died for France." That's exactly how we felt at the start of every goddamn new day on the front line. So we heroically held our positions.

In a trench, like anywhere else, there's always some asshole who'll fuck things up.

On this morning, it was Galipot. He was manning the lookout when he saw two Boches cutting barbed wire under cover of the fog.

Nobody'd asked that fucker Galipot to get one in his crosshairs.

The reply wasn't long in coming.

21

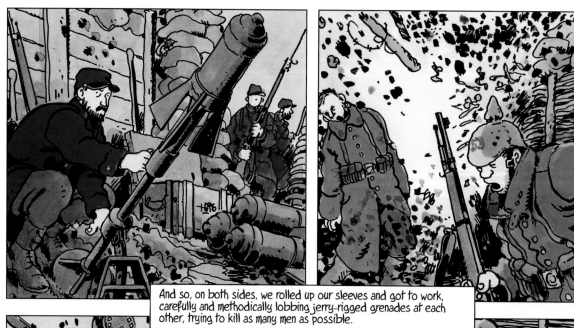

And so, on both sides, we rolled up our sleeves and got to work, carefully and methodically lobbing jerry-rigged grenades at each other, trying to kill as many men as possible.

The fog lifted. Ideal conditions for an outing.

Suddenly the Boches showed up, with no artillery preparation, in a kind of surprise attack to avenge their wire cutters. Nobody wanted to, but we had to go meet them.

Up ahead, I could see Corporal Morille, a sweet guy who'd proudly showed me a photo of his two daughters the night before. He was plunging his bayonet into a young Kraut's chest. I also saw the lieutenant, a tax collector in civilian life, finish off his second Hun with his revolver.

In peacetime, our heads would've rolled for the murders we were now legally required to commit.

Brutality seemed to blaze up from the hellish depths of humanity like a great fire, subsiding only long enough for the dead to be buried before flaring up again.

Our rookie was killed on the spot. No return-ticket wound for him. Boulier got one, though: he'd be walking on a peg leg from now on, but far away from here, on the boulevards. ...Lucky bastard.

The rookie'd joined us eight days ago, in early March. Brugnon'd taken him under his wing. I'd hardly spoken two words to him, but the kid's death got to me. Kid?... He was just two years younger than me. After six months of war, our faces had aged twenty years and we looked like bloodthirsty, hardened old bandits.

When you don't have much education and you've only ever worked at Biscorne on rue des Panoyaux, it takes a while for shit to sink in. But I was starting to get the picture. We'd become beasts, a herd of brutes accustomed to the sight of horrible wounds, exposed entrails and dismembered bodies... It hadn't always been like that.

One morning, in an isolated passageway, we found Cloutier sucking on his rifle. It had gotten to him... When you can't see the end of the tunnel, when you're in an utter shithole, when you feel like you've been handed a life sentence, and that you'll never see your girl again, and that you could be blown to bits by a shell at any moment, it doesn't take much to make you want to leave your buddies and put it all behind you. Then again, maybe Cloutier'd just gotten tired of fighting with an enfrenching shovel.

After eight days on the front line, we were relieved. Weapons drills awaited us back in the rear. Truth to tell, we needed them. After the chaos of trench life, we could use some straightening out and discipline. On our way there, we crossed subjects of His Majesty the King of England, on their way to the front.

The British wanted their colonial subjects to do their part for the war effort. After all, the Brits had brought them education and all the benefits of a superior culture. It was only decent — a little something in return... Giving isn't just a one-way street, after all.

Nor had good old France hesitated to mobilize its North African and black colonial troops. Our Senegalese came from far away. It had taken a while to bring them over, crammed into the holds of cargo ships, to perish in the cold and the mud. But in its boundless generosity, the Republic was proud to offer them the singular honor of dying for the Fatherland.

I wondered how my sleeping Boche was doing — the one in the woods whose crapping friend had been skewered by the dragoons. Was he dead?... Imprisoned?... Hospitalized?

Mail got handed out around the field kitchen. And then the cooks, who always knew the score, told us that the battalion was getting its first six-day leave. The barber had his hands full!

We discovered that civilians were were put off by us stinking, dirty soldiers. They called us "poilus" — hairy ones. They made us travel separately, so as not to offend anyone.

Paris was crawling with rear-echelon fuckers you had to salute. They strutted around with pretty nurses on their arms, showing off their war wounds, which they probably got from knocking over an ink pot in some ministry. There were lots of cripples, widows and orphans...

I'd gotten out of my uniform as fast as possible. I couldn't work up the courage to go see my mother, but I dropped in on Louise at the shop where she worked, and then I settled into a little bar on rue de Panoyaux, not far from the Biscome factory. Somebody told me the owner's kid had lost both his legs at Charleroi. I couldn't get up the nerve to visit the place after that.

The leave zipped right by. We were so terrifically glad to get back to our own little section of the trench, with all its happy memories, that we wouldn't have traded places with anybody.

The lazy bastards who'd filled in while we were away hadn't managed to nibble away so much as an inch of garden soil in the direction of Berlin.

We found out that Brugnon hadn't come back from leave. He'd hanged himself in the stairwell of his building, on rue des Gâtines. He left a note to say he couldn't take it any more and asked us to count him out. We accepted it... Who were we to judge?

Besides, how many men had died while we were taking it easy back home? The chaplain's pathetic theatrics only made the situation more grotesque.

Marked for sacrifice like we were, we started getting crazy ideas... Foolproof schemes for escaping the slaughterhouse. A few guys drank boiling sardine oil: it gave them jaundice and a couple days off in the infirmary. Then there was the whole gamut of self-mutilation. That could be a ticket out of hell, provided you left an arm or a leg behind. I've got to admit I considered blowing off a thumb, but some of the docs were squealers and would turn you over to the firing squad for sure.

We might've had some clever ideas for getting out of the carnage, but the murderers who wanted our skins weren't sleeping either. Gas alert!

On quiet days, we watched the planes overhead. We thought they had it good up there, high above all the crap and the clouds of gas.

Poor old Punch, hung out to dry in the sun.

The attacks kept up, and yet somehow I survived. Chlorine alert!

In May, Italy declared war on the Central Powers. It had taken its time to pick sides, which was understandable.

In July, we were issued steel helmets and new blue uniforms. It was a nice gesture, but we didn't look any better than before.

Poor guy, dead for nothing, rotting in a tangle of wire.

We listened to the blows of pickaxes, hoping the relief party would get us out of the rat hole we were in. Vauquois was the name of the place.

The village of Vauquois had been eaten up from below till there was nothing left of it. This was the so-called "mining war."

Tons of explosives going off under your ass — not a fun experience, believe me.

It was the relief troops that got swallowed up in the bottom of a giant crater.

We'd scrambled out of there in a big hurry. The poor bastards who replaced us heard the pickaxes too, then nothing, followed by a massive blast, and nothing again. Vauquois, that's what the place was called.

In November, I thought I saw my German buddy again — the guy snoring in the woods. Suddenly, we were face to face. We took aim, idiotically, like little kids, but the situation was just too absurd. We both turned away without shooting and headed back to our respective sides. I was glad I didn't kill anybody that day. And I was glad that nobody'd killed me.

We had second thoughts about the planes.

On the front line, it looked like there was no end in sight for this goddamn war.

1916

Our world had turned thoroughly alien. In the giant cauldron we were in, we struggled to hold ridiculous positions in the middle of a refuse heap — an open-air morgue of sorts.

We waited for nightfall to bury our buddies and hoped we wouldn't be trapped by a flare, like the moving targets you shoot in country-fair games to win a pound of sugar or a basket of produce.

Snow fell in January. It covered things up nicely, although sometimes pieces of human flesh settled like red snowflakes on the terrible shroud of the battlefield.

We froze our balls off. You can't imagine the state of our feet, or the stench that emanated from our hides. Our stomachs would churn as we waited for our grub. At the best of times, it was muddy when it got to us. That meant the mess detail had hit the ground in a passageway, knocking over the chow buckets. At worst, the soup was lost in transit, seasoned with shrapnel, and we wrote it off.

The Boches had finally gotten themselves some steel headgear too. The first time I saw one of their helmets was later, during battle, on the skull of the corpse of a tall young Kraut who'd been cut in half.

Our division was ordered to a new sector. When some poor reservists came to replace us in the trenches, we figured out that fresh meat was needed elsewhere, and naturally, they'd thought of us.

The Tommies wore a pressed-steel shaving dish on their noggins, the so-called "Brodie." They were preparing a "decisive offensive."

The Huns, they said, were going to be crushed, annihilated, wiped out, and the war would be over. It would be a magnificent offensive and we would be part of it, too. Just the thought of it made our hearts soar.

On February 21, the Germans started hammering away at a village that had strategic and symbolic value, apparently. I wouldn't've paid a cent to visit that shithole, but the Kaiser's son was dead set on going in, once he'd wrecked the place.

The civilians had fled. Boche shells pounded the town and its garrison, which was hidden away in the citadel. The subprefecture wasn't much to look at any more, with the contents of its pathetic little shacks spilling into the Meuse River.

That's what we were being sent to die for: the defense of a ruined town. Any charm it might've held at one time was now long gone.

VERDUN
5 Km

Traffic on the roads leading to the massacre was dense, and the territorials[1] were having a hell of a time keeping all the roads to the abattoirs open. It took huge amounts of human labor to supply the slaughter with its full allotment of corpses every day. The road crews in this Hell were manned by those too old to join in the mass killings.

One of those old guys, Godet, had an aviator son, and of course he was worried sick about the kid. I chatted with Godet once or twice.

When the kid's biplane got hit and he started burning from the feet on up, he barely had enough time to put a bullet in his head before the plane crashed.

[1] Territorials: reservists assigned to build and maintain roads, railway lines and trench systems.

A Kraut zeppelin more than 200 yards long had somehow strayed into the airspace over the combat zone. It was on it's way back from a bombing mission — over Paris or London — to kill civilians in their sleep, tucked away in their beds. The "kolossal" airship made the mistake of passing directly over a self-propelled anti-aircraft 75, and it's gunlayer took great pleasure in flambéing that massive lost banana, along with it's hydrogen load.

The offensive had begun. The Boche seemed intent on passing through Verdun. We were there to block 'em. The name Bois des Caures probably doesn't mean much to you... Galipot, Morille, Fluet, Flêtan and many more got left behind there, for nothing at all.

The Germans covered up their artillery to hide it from French aircraft.

I ran into my Fritz from the woods again. He was clinging to the side of a shell hole, deader than dead. So he hadn't ended his war in a hospital or POW camp after all. How about me? How was I going to come out of this fucking war? What shape would my mug be in by the end of it?

The French covered up their artillery to hide it from German aircraft.

Some guys would meekly let themselves be led to aid stations, with no eyes, no face, no mouth or tongue, holding in their entrails with their hands, unable to utter more than pitiful groans.

And there were those, far more numerous, who remained on the battlefield. Raoul was one — I barely recognized him. In civilian life, he did deliveries for the Nicolas wine stores, so we called him Nectar, but he never touched a drop. The regiment's drinkers always teased him about it.

We weren't too fond of Raoul. He was consumed by remorse. "I've killed a man," he told the chaplain. And the devil-dodger replied, "You did your duty as a Frenchman before God and man. All the more reason to have a drink!" But Raoul never got over it, and one day he popped his head up above the parapet. He didn't have to wait long for a stick grenade to finish him off.

It's true: he didn't get much comfort from the chaplain, nor from the rest of us, either. On the other hand, Raoul's blunder cost the life of Fluet, who got mowed down by a German in the Bois de Caures. I barely recognized Raoul...

They called it the Sacred Way. Why not the Holy and Glorious Rose-Strewn and Incense-Scented Path to Paradise? The more pious the name, the more atrocious the sacrifice and the surer our place at the side of the Lord, in clouds of phosgene gas. ...That religious crap has always made me want to puke into the holy water.

Sacred Way — my ass! It was a conveyor belt to military cemeteries.

The descendants of your "Gaul ancestors" gave you tools and made you slaves on your own soil. Today, they've brought you here, given you a rifle and ordered you to kill as many barbarian Boches as you can. You might get killed yourself, all for their benefit, but if you do your job, you'll have a nice bronze Cross of War to show for it.

Now that you've been taken prisoner, the Germans don't mistreat you. Instead, they study you out of the corner of their eyes. They're a bit afraid of you, this "savage" bearer of French culture. The head hunter and cutter of German ears. What do they mean when they ask you who the real barbarians are? Maybe they want to turn you against your masters, those "guardians of civilization" with no scruples who sent you into the carnage of this war.

The war wasted no time industrializing itself, and huge profits were raked in over our dead bodies.

Automobiles, planes, motorcycles, trucks, observation balloons and big guns... Isn't progress amazing? We'd stepped squarely into the 20th century and there was no way back. We might as well have stepped straight into our own graves.

In February, Fort Douaumont, which had been stripped of its weapons like the twenty other forts "defending" Verdun, was taken by the Germans. They walked right onto it. Not a single shot was fired.

The forty or so old territorials holding Douaumont were playing cards when the Boches showed up.

BETTER TO BE BURIED BENEATH THE RUINS OF THE FORT THAN SURRENDER

It wasn't until three months later that we found out that a Fritz, reheating his potatoes and sauerkraut in the infirmary, caused a monstrous explosion that pulverized 800 of his comrades. Bronzier thought a monument should be built in his honor. Gustave figured this valiant servant of the "clown prince" had been working for our side. Good old Gustave — he really meant it.

And then came summer, and the Tommies launched their big offensive in the Somme.

The priests called the Brits "virgin roasters" because they'd burned Joan of Arc. Now the virgin roasters wanted to fry themselves some Hun. For help, they called on Australians, New Zealanders, Indians and Canadians, including the French-speaking "Canayens." A big crowd. They all got busy with artillery preparation.

We gave the Brits a hand, just to be part of the show. But we didn't have much to offer. Verdun had taken a lot out of us.

Our "age-old enemies," as our teachers had called them, were intent on breaking through the line of the enemy we shared. All I knew was that personally, I had no enemies at all in this whole business, and I thought it was a bit much that I'd been sent where I was.

The Limeys pulled a surprise out of their sleeve: a state-of-the-art weapon, in which they took great pride.

In 100 days, the Germans covered less than 2 miles in the Douaumont-Vaux sector, which tells you how fierce the fighting was. We went out of our way to make their stay unpleasant.

At little Fort Vaux, the battle raged above- and below-ground, in tunnels, ditches, caponiers and bunkers. The men fought with grenades, machine guns, gas, flame throwers, bayonets and their bare hands. After a five-day siege, the poor bastards trapped inside this stinking tomb couldn't take it any more. Having run out of water, they were reduced to drinking their own piss and finally surrendered. The sitting ducks of Fort Vaux, that was them... Better them than us.

The big brass weren't stingy when it came to spending human lives and shells. Out of necessity or stubbornness, they ordered our massive rail-mounted guns to destroy Vaux and Douaumont so France could recapture its magnificent fortresses, costly and useless though they were. And that's not to mention the other forts in the region!

Fort Vaux, thoroughly destroyed, was recaptured in November. It was in ruins, but it would now be forever French, from the walls of its moat to its air shafts.

The Germans failed to get past Verdun, and the British failed to break through at the Somme.

At the end of the year, I received a letter from Louise that got past the censors without difficulty. She was working at the Puteaux Arsenal, making shells. It was her war effort, as she put it.

She'd left her boss and the flower shop at Place Gambetta. Of course, Louise didn't have a clue. You couldn't understand if you hadn't been here...

And the war continued...

1917

"Never before had a commander held greater power than the *generalissimo* in 1914!
And never had a commander responded so weakly to the expectations placed upon him."
Henri MELOT, Brevet Lieutenant-Colonel MELOT, *The Truth About the War*

"The experience is conclusive. Victory is certain, I assure you of that.
Germany will learn it at her expense."
Robert NIVELLE, the new *generalissimo,* December 15, 1916

You got used to it, but it still wasn't pretty to see what you'd most likely look like at the end of the day.

"All your life, you keep your trap shut. The only time you get to open it is when you die," Lucien said to me between gushes of bloody drool spewing from his mouth and nostrils. It was near the "lost village of Vauquois," as he lay dying in my arms. He howled himself hoarse as he searched for his stomach, which was no longer there.

The Germans were pulling back, but only to shorten their line and strengthen their positions. They'd done it before. On their way out, they leveled every last shed. All they left behind was booby-trapped roads and poisoned wells. You had to be fucking careful where you walked. And you wanted to drink nothing but wine.

So we were face to face with the Boches again, only a bit further down the road and a short while later. It was like this goddamn war was never going to end.

There was slaughter at sea, too, or so we heard. The losses were recorded in tons. But from one periscope to the next, the target was always the same. It was always the same idea and the same poor bastard that was being obliterated in the name of the fatherland... And we were all screwed, because every one of us was the child of a fatherland.

Over in their trenches, the Germans were getting wiped out "for the fatherland" as well. Except they were dying with empty bellies. People were eating nothing but turnips in Berlin, but since the Kaiser himself wasn't queuing up for potatoes yet, the war went on.

We poured a shot of wine into a guy we'd tried to kill a few minutes earlier and who'd come over, wounded, to surrender. It was absurd, but it was in the conventions. Sapin would've shot him — a German machine-gunner who'd taken out Frelon and Lamantin.

Sometimes we took no prisoners. That wasn't by the book, but the fact that there were any rules at all where we'd been put was a load of crap to begin with. It was too late for etiquette.

One evening I saw him again — my Boche from the little wood. He pulled me out of a hole I was stuck in. So he hadn't died in Verdun after all. Here he was, along with the rest of us... We couldn't talk because we didn't speak the same language. What a shame.

A ridge lined with artillery and blockhouses: that was our target. We were supposed to charge up the hill — straight into enemy machine gunfire, of course. It was going to be quick and easy, under the April snow. This was the big victory offensive that the old windbag Nivelle had been promising for months. We were in Craonne and you can't imagine a worse place on earth.

Of course, the Senegalese were sent in with the first assault waves. They got mowed down by the thousands, with nothing to show for it.

We were in Craonne and we were getting slammed from all sides.

That was one steep fucking slope! If you were lucky enough to get over the barbed wire, you had to try and climb. The grenades we threw were bouncing down onto our skulls, so we turned around fast, only to be sent straight back up.

We went up again and again, without ever managing to set foot on that damned ridge. The valley below was a sea of blue. We waded through spilled entrails. We'd been put in the hands of a pigheaded incompetent — a bigwig within the hierarchy of butchers.

Hidden in their tunnels, the Germans let our assault waves wash over them, waiting to get us from behind.

We saw buddies turn black on the clotheslines. Others called out for stretchers, their mothers or the Virgin Mary. But you can bet that any one of 'em would have preferred to see the general there instead. It was no way to be thinking. Chalk it up to the agony of death — it drove men crazy.

Paulet François, who'd sung the Song of Craonne[1] along with everybody else, was ratted out.

Worse yet, he'd refused to return to the front, because of the strike. The court used the word "mutiny," although no officers had been abused by their men.

Everything Paulet said was used against him. He told them he couldn't take it any more. He told them how discouraged and outraged he felt after the useless and bloody April offensive. But what really hurt his case was his refusal to say who had taught him the words to the song.

When he stepped back into the classroom, he knew his fate was sealed before he even opened his mouth. His "judges" told him: "You're not worthy of being French!" ...As if that even mattered!

There were no mitigating circumstances for Paulet... Others had been luckier. Having completed its unworthy task, the "tribunal" left with a clear conscience, proud to be a part of the French army.

They locked Paulet into a cellar. Two policemen kept watch outside. He'd heard that soldiers had killed a couple of cops after they'd sent a guy to be court-martialed for swiping booze. It warmed his heart to think about it. He refused to see the chaplain and left the food they brought untouched, but since they'd let him keep his tobacco, he rolled a cigarette as he waited for the day to break.

[1] Anti-military song, composed in 1917, popular with the troops. (See page 92)

At dawn, a detachment led Paulet to a wall, where a wooden post had been erected.

Executions were never held in the same place twice, but they must have bent the rules for Paulet, since that post had been used the day before.

They stood in front of the troops. Four soldiers and a sergeant flanked the condemned man. The drums beat a salute. It was all by the book.

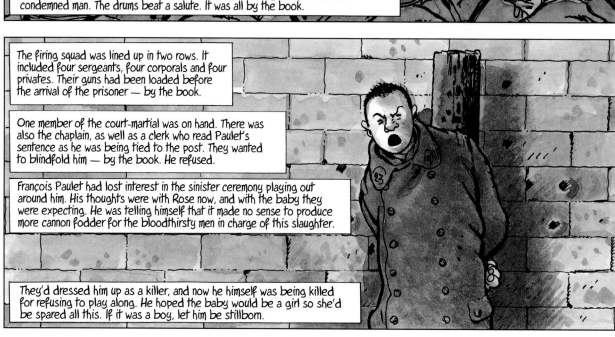

The firing squad was lined up in two rows. It included four sergeants, four corporals and four privates. Their guns had been loaded before the arrival of the prisoner — by the book.

One member of the court-martial was on hand. There was also the chaplain, as well as a clerk who read Paulet's sentence as he was being tied to the post. They wanted to blindfold him — by the book. He refused.

François Paulet had lost interest in the sinister ceremony playing out around him. His thoughts were with Rose now, and with the baby they were expecting. He was telling himself that it made no sense to produce more cannon fodder for the bloodthirsty men in charge of this slaughter.

They'd dressed him up as a killer, and now he himself was being killed for refusing to play along. He hoped the baby would be a girl so she'd be spared all this. If it was a boy, let him be stillborn.

The platoon took position 20 feet in front of the condemned man. The sergeant major assumed his position four paces to the right and two paces in front of him. He lifted his sword. The twelve men took aim at the middle of the prisoner's chest — by the book. Paulet wondered if it was true that one of the rifles was loaded with a blank round. The sergeant major gave the firing squad a moment to line up their shots. "Aim true or he'll only suffer more." FIRE!

What we should've done is load our rifles and shoot our commanders instead. Now that would've been a mutiny worth writing home about. Imagine if the Germans had done the same thing on their side. Instead, we watched François Paulet's execution without moving a muscle. I wasn't proud of myself at that moment.

An NCO delivered the coup de grâce, placing the barrel of his revolver above Paulet's ear, an inch and a half from his skull — by the book.

We all had to file past Paulet's body. A few of the men muttered: "Died for France. We will avenge you." We all sang the Song of Craonne under our breaths.

General Nivelle cut a helluva fine figure in uniform. Especially when you consider all the men who didn't, and who died for having worn one.

Once the "mutinies" had been squashed, the army rations improved (salad, Gruyère and chocolate), leave was re-established, the general was sacked, and we finally captured that goddamn ridge. It took us seven months. In 1918, the Germans would take it back in just twenty-four hours!

The distance from Craonne to the Chemin des Dames isn't far. But it took us a hell of a long time to cover it, and we lost a lot of buddies along the way.

Chemin des Dames — the Ladies' Road. Pretty name...

The Russians stationed in France didn't feel like fighting any more. The officers lost control of the men, and soon we had to pull them from the front and send them to a camp in La Courtine, in the Creuse region. Me, a lathe worker at Biscorne, on Rue des Panoyaux, I would have gladly gone all the way to Moscow to see what a real revolution looked like. I sure didn't belong here, singing the Internationale with the rest of them as we let ourselves be led to the slaughterhouse.

The war, which had been waged underground at Vauquois, was being fought on the heights of the Alps.

A vertical battle pitted the Italians against the Austrians, who were starving up in the mountains.

The Italians also sent men to the firing squad "to set an example." I couldn't make up my mind which was more appalling: the mining war or the mountain war. And between an Italian general and a French one, I wouldn't've known which one to shoot first.

Come September, the Brits were getting slammed at Passchendaele, in Belgian Flanders.

The troops in that sludge weren't professionals. They were conscripts, sent to die in the cold rain and mud.

To make up for losses, the army had dropped the height requirement for its future casualties to 5 feet, and special battalions of short soldiers had been formed since the start of the war. I'd seen some of them. "Bantams" is what they called them, after a breed of small fighting roosters.

The Bantams, who tired quickly, weren't cut out to be killers. They were treated as inferiors. Some were executed. I swear, I couldn't tell who were the bigger bastards, the British generals or the French ones. I still haven't figured it out.

The tea water didn't always arrive at its destination on time.

The Germans persevered stubbornly.

The Tommies floundered methodically.

The Americans, who'd arrived by the boatload in late June, were finally sent into the field in November. The war was really in for it now! Coming to France was like traveling back a few centuries in time for those lucky bastards. They scrubbed down, naked, at the pump in the godforsaken village where we'd billeted them. They had toilet paper, and they even brushed their teeth, which scared the hell out of the local peasants. They were an expeditionary corps among swine.

Uncle Sam's boys might as well've brought out glass trinkets and salt to trade with the natives. They were real friendly, especially with the grandmothers, kids and young women. It was hard to know what they thought of the broken down Europe they'd found... After all, they came from the same manure heap we did.

While the Sammies were being trained to lasso the Germans, it was business as usual for the rest of us.

The war was eating us alive, and hunkered down within the stench of our miserable existence, I clung to a single hope: I just wanted to get home, and to hell with winning or losing this war that wasn't mine to begin with. Get home and stay out of the mass graves dug by the Tonkinese work crews.

In December, we were given a six-day furlough.

61

1918

It was a strange place for a country picnic. The stretcher bearers were taking a break in the midst of the carnage. These guys, who saw the suffering of both sides day and night, who tended to horrendous wounds in bodies torn open, blown apart, perforated and mangled, who had to put up with moans, cries and screams of pain and agony — these guys sometimes came under sniper fire. Those who knew the game would ask the dying for money to bring their bodies back from no man's land. But that was rare.

I thought of what Louise had told me about my boss when I was on leave. He'd started looking out for himself, too. He was welding canisters for gas masks and making a killing. If I got out of this war alive, no way would I go back to slave away at Biscorne, on Rue des Panoyaux.

In March, the Germans mounted a surprise attack — a lightning advance! We weren't about to let them get by, though, not after all the trouble we'd gone to. But then the Brits got it full in the face in Picardy. It was Waterloo all over again.

Try as we might, we couldn't stop the Huns, as the Brits liked to call them. It was the Battle of Trafalgar! Except this time, the Brits were as deep in the shit as we were!

The Germans bombed Paris and London too. Huddled in their beds, the civvies were seeing their share of the action.

And then another goddamn surprise. A cluster of long-range guns located about 60 miles from rue de Panoyaux began raining shells on the center of Paris. Nobody knew exactly where they were firing from. I didn't really care if they wrecked Notre Dame. It's not like the church was doing much, except fanning the flames of an ideological holy war.

Other guns were hammering our positions. Everything seemed to be gaining in intensity, like one last vicious burst of energy. They were kicking us in the balls, one blast after another.

It wasn't a war about "justice," that's for sure. Nobody was saving civilization. It was a war to protect the interests of all those big guys whose treasure chests were already overflowing: Schneider, St. Chamond, Fiat, Krupp, Vickers, Renault, A.E.G., Fokker, Hotchkiss and the others, and now Biscorne, too!

The Sammies brought typewriters, bathtubs, soap, lawnmowers, ambulances, medicine for the clap and trains, but not a single cannon, plane, vehicle or machine gun. They fought with material supplied by us and the Brits.

They did bring along the slaves we'd sold them a while back to work the cotton fields in the South. But they didn't arm their black soldiers properly. They didn't want to turn them into battle heroes, in case it went to their heads once the bloodshed was over. They wanted them digging ditches or driving mules. At least we stuck our colonial troops in the front lines where they could die for France. We did make them all kinds of promises that we had no plans to keep, of course.

The Americans were totally green and their sector was in chaos. Ambulances loaded to bursting waited for hours, like cabs in a New York traffic jam.

The war was destined to go on and on. And once it was done, there'd be others. People called it the "war to end all wars." Bullshit. It had been like this since the dawn of man, whether the fight was over fire, bananas or oil. And it was always the same old song — to the tune of human bones being tossed into the meat grinder. Why should it change now?

The Germans were advancing. Paris was threatened. And there we were again, on the banks of the Marne. If my German buddy from the little wood was still alive, why not here? It might stir up some memories for him.

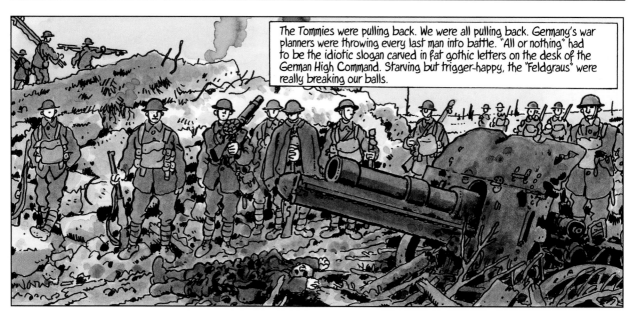

The Tommies were pulling back. We were all pulling back. Germany's war planners were throwing every last man into battle. "All or nothing" had to be the idiotic slogan carved in fat gothic letters on the desk of the German High Command. Starving but trigger-happy, the "Feldgraus" were really breaking our balls.

And then we were back at the Chemin des Dames, which the Germans had just taken from us again. What a fucking fiasco! We'd suffered so much in this place just a year ago. Had it even been worth it?

The Scots went into battle bare-assed and bloody-kneed, playing their bagpipes like this was some folkloric killing game, all for the greater glory of the British Empire.

It was a lousy idea to take the fight into the air, drawing light, graceful figures in the sky that cast a spell on those of us below, ankle-deep in mud.

The squadron's top dog inevitably finished his spiral on the ground, burned alive in his crate before he could blow his brains out. A pretty fiancée somewhere would shed a few tears for the handsome young flying ace, who had just written a heroic and brand new page in the history of warfare.

In June, America's elite forces got their baptism by fire in Belleau Wood. But in the end, the Germans couldn't hold out.

Berlu got himself killed while he was taking a crap. Decapitated by a shell fragment. He died clutching his ass-scratcher, on which he'd carved the Holy Cross of Jesus, protector of France and the poilus. The poor bastard didn't even have time to wipe himself.

In September, it was back to the Chemin des Dames. There was no getting away from it! But this time it was the Germans that got kicked out. The Sammies were advancing in Argonne, the Tommies in the north and us in Champagne. The retreat had changed sides. We even saw a few Italians, who'd apparently come to lend a hand.

This was the big Allied advance, but there were still a few hold-outs to deal with on the way to Berlin. One thousand five hundred days — that's how long my beer had been waiting for me on some café table by the Alexanderplatz... It was probably flat by now. Or maybe someone else had drunk it?

It wasn't time yet to sit back and tell our grandkids about the war we'd fought. But would we even want to talk about this appalling carnage, this sickening mass suicide?

The Boches were yelling "Kamerad!" That's what both sides should have done from the start, to avoid the massacres organized by the higher-ups. But they'd shoved rifles in our hands, so we had to use them, and things had just gone on from there.

When we heard the Spanish flu was taking countless civilian lives, we told ourselves we were better off where we were.

We were chasing the Germans, and suddenly we found ourselves in untouched countryside. The trees had leaves here, and it made me think of the little lieutenant from the start of the war. Four years had passed since he bit the dust after ordering that reckless attack. I'd managed to save my ass since that August day, and this wasn't the time to fuck up.

A couple of our guys still had the strength to fire their weapons, like Feugerolles, whose wife and kids had spent the entire time in occupied territory. He'd never received a single word from them. Had they been separated? Had his wife been dragged to Germany to help make the shells that rained down on us? Had she shacked up with a Bavarian? You could understand the rage that had him shooting the German rear guard troops in the back. Nobody bothered with big principles any more. We'd been turned into assassins, granted total impunity.

The last time I saw Collin was in 1917, at the foot of Mort-Homme.

Before the great slaughter, Collin'd been an avid angler. On that day, he was standing at the hole, watching maggots swarm among blow flies on two bodies that we couldn't retrieve for burial without putting our own lives at risk.

And there, at the loop hole, he thought of his bamboo rods, his flies and the new reel he hadn't even tried out yet.

Collin was imagining himself on the riverbank, wine cooling in the current, his stash of worms in a little metal box and a maggot on his hook, writhing like... Holy shit. Were the corpses getting to him?

Collin. The poor guy didn't even have time to sort out his thoughts.

In that split second, he was turned into a slab of bloody meat. A white hot hook drilled right through him and churned through his guts, which spilled out of a hole in his belly.

He was cleared out of the first aid station. The major did triage. Stomach wounds weren't worth the trouble. They were all going to die anyway, and besides, he wasn't equipped to deal with them.

Behind the aid station, next to a pile of wood crosses, there was a heap of body parts and shapeless, oozing human debris laid out on stretchers, stirred only by passing rats and clusters of large white maggots.

But on their last run, the stretcher bearers carried him out after all... Old Collin was still alive.

From the aid station to the ambulance and from the ambulance to the hospital, all he could remember was his fall into that pit, with maggots swarming over the open wound he had become from head to toe... Come to think of it, where was his head? And what about his feet?

In the ambulance, the bumps were so awful and the pain so intense that it would have been a relief to pass out. But he didn't. He was still alive, writhing on his hook.

72

They carved up old Collin good. They fixed him as best they could, but his hands and legs were gone. So much for fishing.

Later, they pinned a medal on him, right there in that putrid recovery room.

And later still, they explained to him about gangrene and bandages packed with larvae that feed on dead tissue. He owed them his life. From one amputation and operation to the next — thirty-eight in all — the docs finally got him "back up on his feet." But by then, the war was long over.

The Armistice was signed on the eleventh hour of the eleventh day of the eleventh month of the year 1918. This was not peace yet, but we weren't fussy. It was high time. My German buddy and me, we couldn't take it any more. Our tormenters were taking a break. The sudden silence was deafening. There wasn't even a distant drumroll of gunfire to give our ears some relief.

Some of our guys began to rush over to the Germans, who were coming toward us as well. But the officers in our sector maintained discipline and kept the two sides apart. The flares that were shot into the sky that night created a spectacular fireworks display along the entire front. But the war could start up again at any moment.

The last Germans, who'd stayed in position to slow us down right through to the end, took their leave of us. It was the first time we saw them from behind. They retreated in an orderly manner, weapons and bags in hand. The war could flare up again like a poorly extinguished fire. This was no time for foolishness.

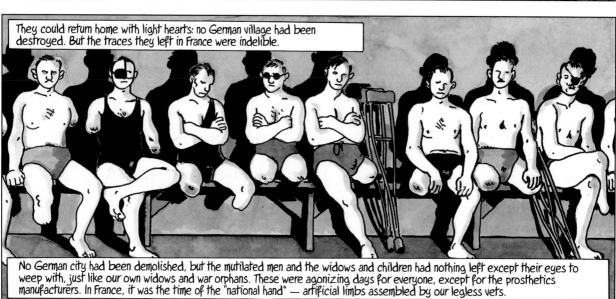

They could return home with light hearts: no German village had been destroyed. But the traces they left in France were indelible.

No German city had been demolished, but the mutilated men and the widows and children had nothing left except their eyes to weep with, just like our own widows and war orphans. These were agonizing days for everyone, except for the prosthetics manufacturers. In France, it was the time of the "national hand" — artificial limbs assembled by our legless vets.

Why were the men displayed naked — those men forever broken by fear? It was called "shell shock" and they were suspected of being fakers. Why put the men on display like this? In the name of science or humiliation? In December, the Nobel Prize in Chemistry was awarded to the German chemist who had dedicated four years to perfecting the production of poison gas.

It was a laugh — at our expense. The trick they pulled on us made me bitter, and no war cross can lessen my hatred for you, "all-merciful Lord."

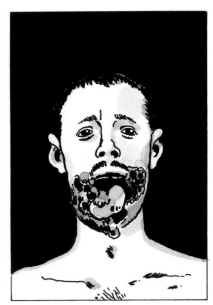
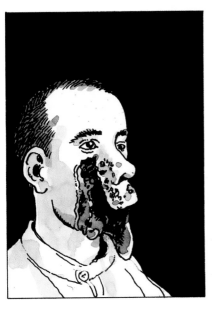

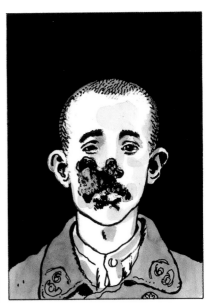

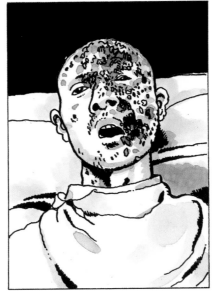
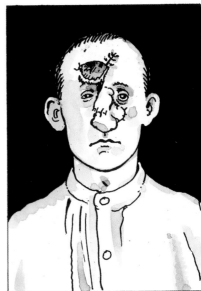

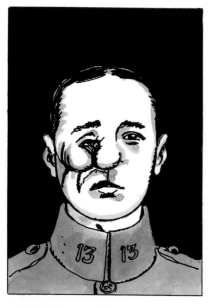
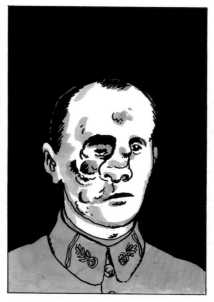
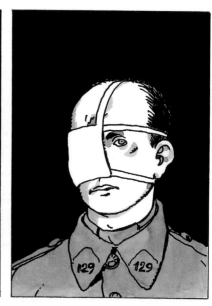
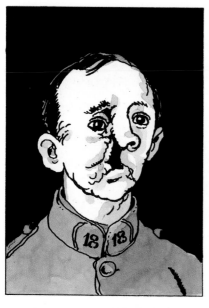
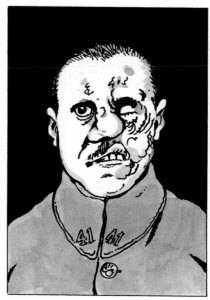
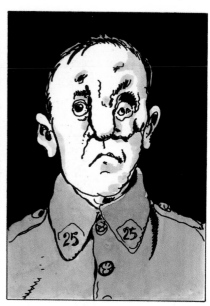

1919

*"The European war, which later spread to the world, was a terrible event:
no principle, thought, or great idea illuminated it."*
Francesco NITTI, Prime Minister of Italy (1919-1920)

"We civilizations now know that we are mortal."
Paul VALÉRY

You're evacuating your brother and sister on your own. Your parents are dead. The sound of the cannon hidden in the wood terrified you, so you decided to get away from the nearby combat zone. It'll be slow going, but you'll manage to get to Paris on foot with both kids. You've got the address of an aunt who's a concierge and she'll put you up in her small apartment. In the end, though, a shell fired by that same huge cannon in the wood, more than 60 miles away, will kill all three of you in your aunt's concierge apartment on Rue des Martyres.

You fire off all your rounds as fast as you can so you'll have to hunker down. Maybe you'll even leave this old sewing machine in the field... Damn thing's so heavy! You're not stupid enough to play the hero and die in combat for no reason like Potard, who's bleeding out next to you. You know you wouldn't be right for the role, with a bullet in your skull and your tail between your legs.

In civilian life, you're a clockmaker in Cologne, and you're feeling desperate in this rotten corner of France. God knows why, but all hell's going to break loose here in twenty seconds. The shells will spare you and you'll be captured by Algerian infantry, who'll tear off your epaulettes for souvenirs. You'll have been very scared, but lucky, too. It wasn't your time yet.

You've started this letter to your *marraine de guerre*[1] at least five times already. She sent you her photo and you don't know how to go about it any more. There's so much to say and it's so difficult to put down on paper — it's all too hard.

It's too complicated for a simple infantryman who's barely literate and just smart enough to take orders. Soon you'll go back to the front and you won't even have time to pass the note you finally finished into the hands of the postal clerk.

You stayed there under fire for four days, by your buddy, using a long stick to reach biscuits to his mouth. Ropes couldn't get him out of the shell hole he was caught in without killing him. You two had grown up in the same neighborhood, you'd worked in the same factory, you'd enlisted on the same day. When your buddy swallowed his last mouthful of Belgian mud, you lost it, and your mind never really came back from Passchendaele.

[1] "Wartime godmother." The *marraines de guerre* were women who volunteered to write letters to the troops, to boost their morale.

Why'd you come out of your hole? You could've pissed inside that stinking rat's nest, it wouldn't have made any difference. You'll never finish the game of cards you were playing... Three pieces of shrapnel will pierce your helmet and skull. The place will live up to its name: the Ravine of Death.

You tremble in the arms of the German doctor. He seems kind enough, he's bandaged you with care, but you can't bring yourself to really trust him. You know white people, and you know they've never done anything good for you. First they beat you to make you work, then they forced you to come here and fight for them in the cold. What will they do to you now?

The Germans don't understand how "civilized" nations can let savages fight their wars. And yet, the "civilized" nations themselves are behaving like savages!

Playing with knives and drinking — those are the specialties of the "volunteers" they've brought in to help. And all with extensive criminal records to boot. The chaplain performs a quick absolution. That only makes sense, given what needs to be done: breach the line in order to take a few prisoners and force them to talk, in case one of them is privy to the Kaiser's secret plans. And if the Germans catch wind of your mission and run off, so much the better. You'll hightail it back and bullshit the captain about the ten Boches whose throats you slit when they refused to surrender... You'll bring along a German entrenching tool or mess tin as proof. What a fine trench cleaner you are! You'll get four days of leave to kick back with the liquor you pilfered from the infirmary... A job well done!

"Attrition warfare" only added to the casualties, thanks to the useless devices churned out by the Office of Inventions.

It was an unbelievable display of military stupidity, French-style... And of course, you paid the price for it.

You built dead trees out of papier maché, as well as fake cannons, fake bodies, plaster rocks, dummy periscopes to observe those on the other side and wooden railroad tracks to fool aerial surveillance. You molded things, painted them piss yellow, shit brown and spinach green... The camouflage section was like a toy shop. The only thing missing were the little toy soldiers.

Before the war, you wrote cheap adventure novels whose storylines didn't really hold together. Here, you kept a diary in a notebook that you hid away. A daily record of our miserable lives. It was real life, with a solid plot... And then a shell cut you in two. We never found your notebook. It disappeared, and with it, all the misery you'd consigned to paper — all our despair, our suffering, our cries of pain and our stories. All lost, as if they were forever sealed in a bottle tossed into a sea of blood and sludge.

You had orders to film the destruction caused by the German vandals, the horror show of the armies, Sunday mass, the healthy and happy outdoor life of the poilus, reconstructions of magnificent battles, and jolly, well-fed generals throwing back bad red wine — benevolent regimental leaders surrounded by soldiers at the field kitchen. And also German corpses, which were more decorative than ours, to comfort the mothers. You were a propaganda tool. We were all heroes in the official photographs authorized by the censors.

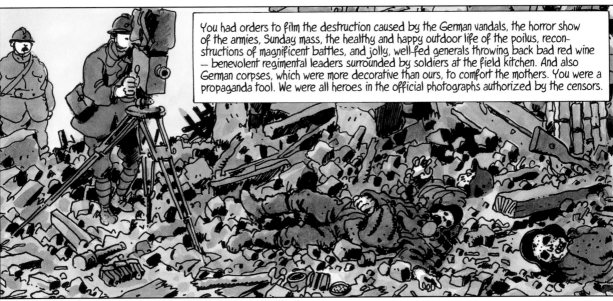

Father, you'd head out on your own with your pilgrim's staff and a gun. We didn't know what you were up to. The guys said you sometimes liked to fire at the Boches while reciting last rites... It could be... We never knew. "If Jesus was alive, he'd take a French gun and shoot the Germans," you used to say to whoever would listen. One evening, you walked off into Hell, and we never saw you again. It was three days before we even noticed you were gone!

Some women work in the fields, others toil away in factories for miserable wages. They make up a large work force, and it seems they're more meticulous, docile and efficient than men... Your husband needs guns, gas and airplanes: get busy! Careful that you don't lose a hand to the machines! At the end of the war, you'll have three months to leave. You need to make way for the men coming back from the trenches. You have no voting rights. Shut up and go home. Why not make a few babies, now that you've made killing machines.

You were too close to the front line! You had no excuse for being there, and your Alsatian accent did you in. Tried, found guilty of espionage and executed, all in no time and out of sight. Just a splash of peasant blood on the snow...

Cutting tunnels through rock at altitudes of 10,000 ft to undermine the Austrians on the summit (because whoever controls the top, controls the bottom): it doesn't suit you at all. You're at the bottom and your morale isn't any higher, plus you're freezing your balls off and your nerves are shot. You make up your mind: you're going home to the warmth of Agrigento.

Your legs are like noodles, you're coughing up blood and your hands are a pulpy mess. You see the cloud of gas drifting your way but you're unable to slip on your mask! You'll wait, but the stretcher bearers will never come. The fucking bastards — they promised they'd get you, no matter what!

They filmed you in this village in the Vosges because you had a sweet smile and the melancholy gaze of a guy going back up to the line. What was your name? How old were you? What kind of work did you do? What were your dreams? Did you have brothers on the front who were still alive? A mother? A wife? Children? They liked your face: that look of the designated victim, docile and poignant. You must have seemed like the model French soldier, full of noble intentions and expendable, the guy who'd been told that dying for the fatherland is the best anyone can do. Did you believe them? What kind of a shithole did they put you into? You had other things to do in life... Did you come back?

You were celebrating in the Courtyard of the Invalids, General, handing out trinkets to poor bastards with no arms and no legs while hoping your brown-nosing assistant had remembered to book you a nice table at Maxim's.

Little August soldier in your madder-red trousers: you tried to hide but there wasn't much cover behind the poppies. You entered the history books dressed up like a trooper in a comic opera, little August casualty.

You're dying of hunger, and now that you're a prisoner, they have you pose for the photographer holding a loaf of French bread. It's nothing like the German sawdust ersatz you've been eating. Some of the guys are scowling. The smarter ones are happy enough. Let the war manage without them. Very young Feldgraus are smoking cigars, gifts from the Kaiser. Seeing these kids smoke will outrage the Americans, but the fact that a Mauser was put in your hands at puberty won't upset anybody.

You were so traumatized from running through the trenches, with bullets whistling past your helmet and your head drawn down between your shoulders, that you couldn't straighten up again. Doubled over, paralyzed by fear — if you made it out alive, you were doomed to be jolted by the electrodes of the good Dr. Vincent, at Val-de-Grâce Military Hospital.

Strange, because it wasn't your first assault. You'd seen three-quarters of your company fall around you. Plus you were sure you'd pulled the right number. Hadn't you written your mother that you would come out of the war alive? "The Germans haven't made the bullet that can kill me yet..." You liked that line. But now you're hunched up at the bottom of the shelter, hiding. You're not sure of anything any more, you're afraid, you've thrown up. You wet your pants when the first wave went over top. They'll find you sitting in your own crap, green with fear. In the end, it'll be twelve French bullets that kill you.

You've just been taken prisoner and it's all right. It's even better than a self-inflicted return-ticket wound. The others can continue without you, if they feel like it. You get sent to a camp someplace, you don't give a damn where. You've saved your skin and the further you are from the front, the better. You wind up in the town of Dache, in Silesia, pulling up potatoes. You've never worked in the fields and you'll get a sore back. You'll come home worn out, without a second thought for the farm girl you got pregnant, and you'll find your own wife knocked up by a Boche prisoner imprudently assigned to her factory. You'll want to move to a new neighborhood.

You're waiting to be evacuated from a beach in Gallipoli. Dysentery, malaria, dengue fever and the incompetence of your commanders back in London will slow the fall of the Ottoman empire. And in the meantime, the Turks will continue to exterminate the Armenians.

Helmut, your sausage is on fire! You jump from the basket, but your parachute doesn't open in time.

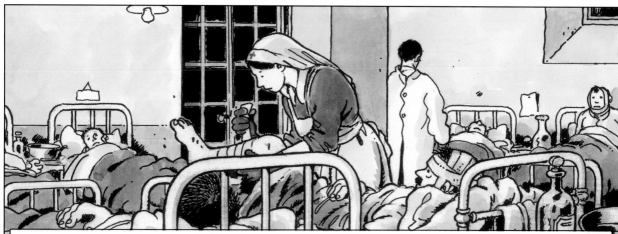

You're swimming in pus, here in this room where you saw your younger brother die. You've watched your mother, so you know how much time and effort it takes to raise a child to adulthood. You remember the infinite patience it took to teach him right from wrong and the worry when he was ill, up until he was old enough to be a soldier and got wiped out in an instant! You comfort the wounded, thinking of your own son, who's just a few months old. There's been no word from his father on the front. Sick with worry, you tend to the dying.

There's no denying that the Brits were the ones with the sea legs. And so the stubborn Limeys, who always liked a naval battle, took their steel armada out into the cold waters of Jutland. Bad move. From that point on, the cheaper and more effective German submarines would rule the sea. The Kaiser didn't want anyone smashing up his beautiful war fleet. He was very fond of his colossal treasures.

You just wanted to forget this whole fucking mess for a moment, so you gave in to the urge to play a few bars of "Tipperary." You couldn't have guessed that your two hands would stay in Cambrai. Who would've thought that the Boches had booby-trapped the piano with a grenade? mi fa so so so ♪ la si do mi ♪ mi re do la do so ♭

Poor beasts of burden, on the hard cobblestones of the north.

You were lucky to find some floating pieces in the debris of 235,000 tons of scrap iron.

This is your second sortie since you joined the fighter squadron and you've just downed your first Fokker! It'll be officially logged. Time to celebrate. You've always liked speed, so you've got a motorcycle behind the hangar and you race to the mess hall to break out the champagne with the guys. Your plane is doing fine, there's just a couple of tears in the wing, nothing serious. Next time, your motorcycle will stay parked behind the hangar... Your mechanic will keep it to remember you by.

There's not a mean bone in you, but you've just killed one more man. When you found yourself nose to nose with the young Boche, you didn't hesitate! He was quaking in his boots, he didn't look like a bad kid... But you fired without hesitating. You were scared, too. So you shot him. It took a hell of a long time before he finally died at your feet. He had come toward you without his rifle, holding both arms up and shouting, "Kamarad! Kamerad!" "You're a real asshole, aren't you!" said Flocon, who saw you do it. You came close to finishing him off, too — you don't know what held you back. And then you got hit by shrapnel. A minor wound. You'll be back, and you'll eventually make it home.

"Don't be angry, just admire." Those were the words on a sign placed on the ruined façade of the city hall of Péronne. The Germans had sacked the town on their way out. And now you're entering another town, Cambrai. The place is in flames. From Canada to the far end of the Somme: it's been a hell of a trip, and you would gladly have missed it.

You and the other kids work hard at the mine, feeding the blast furnaces that turn out steel for the cannons. Little slave, you need to look well-treated and content. The propaganda officer playfully extracts a smile from you for the camera. This film will be play in all neutral countries so people can see what a children's paradise Germany's occupied territories have become!

It's official: you've lost the war and Germany is under Allied occupation. You find it hard to take off your hat as the funeral procession goes by. The body of a French soldier is being brought to the train station so he can be laid to rest back home, on the other side of the Rhine. It isn't easy to take off your hat: the French killed your son. You were told he died at Hill 304, but his body was never found.

You lost your eyes at the Chemin des Dames. If you could catch a glimpse of the Ministry's little sharpshooters at the front of the parade, it would make you see red — you, who have no eyes left to cry with. You hear the bells and patriotic songs and imagine the dancing and celebration. It's an outpouring of joy, as indecent after four years of war as a bawdy song at the end of a wake.

In Paris, crowds marked the anniversary of the Armistice. You watched the maimed go by and, despite it all, you couldn't help feeling glad that you'd managed to come home with all your teeth. You were so unnerved by the thought that you vowed never to return to the monument for the dead in November. You could see the buddies who hadn't come back as if they were still alive. Gallipot... Potard... Flétan... Morille... Fluet... Cloutier...

You've sorted more than your share of unlucky bastards, scattered about in sticky pieces. You searched them for their identification tags and personal belongings. Desk officers sent form letters to the families: Died for France on... November 17, 1916... at... the sugar mill of (illegible) in Aisne... Cause of death... combat wounds... Born... August 29, 1894. That would have made him 22 years old — my grandfather.... Henri-Maxime-Joseph. Rank... soldier, 149th Infantry Regiment. Unit number: 16330, Recruitment number 878... Class 1914.

Others got treated to a nice monument with a cavernous ossuary in the basement. Atheists and believers alike were lined up in rows under cement crosses... The bronze medals were in the shape of the cross, too.

You got a hero's welcome in Berlin, and now a victory celebration greets you at home. You're covered with flowers, just like when you left for the slaughter. You've come back, a symbol of hope for the future... But first you need to get well again. Dressing up defeat as victory — that's nothing new. When poor suckers get fooled, they need to rebuild their trust. Trust in their country, in a god or in a leader. And pretty soon, you'll be putting your fate in the hands of one of your own, who's been through the hell of the trenches like you. And this war you've fought will have been for nothing!... Of course, a few clear-eyed people will foresee the disasters to come. But for now, Wilhelm is taking it easy in the Netherlands and revolution is spreading through Germany. Things can't go on like this. Order has to be restored, the young German republic needs to assert itself!

And what about my German soldier from the little wood — where is he? Did he get out alive? Is he fighting in the streets of Berlin? On which side — with the Spartacists or the militias? Is he fighting for a better world? Maybe we'll see each other again. Without rifles in our hands, I hope.

I've only got one hand now — the left one. The other one stayed in Argonne. So much for Biscorne. Anyway, I made up my mind that I was done working for him. Yesterday, I met his kid in a wheelchair, being pushed by a lady from the Red Cross. He didn't even recognize me. Louise has gone back to her old job at Place Gambetta... She's selling chrysanthemums.

91

THE SONG OF CRAONNE

Author: unknown. Sung to the tune of Charles Sablon's "Bonsoir M'amour." Translation: K.T.

After a week of leave
It's back to the trenches
We're so useful there
They'd get slammed without us
It's really over now, we've had enough
No one wants to march any more
With heavy hearts and a sob in our throats
It's so long to you civvies
There ain't no drums, there ain't no trumpets
But we're headed that way, our heads hung low

CHORUS:
Farewell to life, farewell to love
Farewell, all you women
It's all over now, forever
This dreadful war
We're supposed to leave our bones
Up in Craonne on that plateau
'Cause we're all doomed
We've all been sacrificed

A week in the trenches, a week of agony
But we're still hoping
For the relief to come
That we've been waiting for
Suddenly in the silent night
We see someone advancing
It's an infantry officer
He's here to replace us
Quietly, in the shadows, under the falling rain
The soldiers go look for their graves

CHORUS:
Farewell to life, farewell to love
Farewell, all you women
It's all over now, forever
This dreadful war
We're supposed to leave our bones
Up in Craonne on that plateau
'Cause we're all doomed
We've all been sacrificed

It's awful to see, on the great boulevards
All those fat cats whooping it up
Life may be sweet for them
But it sure ain't so for us
Instead of hiding, all those shirkers
Ought to climb into the trenches
To defend their wealth, 'cause we've got nothing
Us poor miserable bastards
All our comrades are buried here
Defending these gentlemen's wealth

FINAL CHORUS:
Those who've got the dough, they'll be back
'Cause it's for them that we're dying
But it's over now, 'cause all the grunts
Are gonna go on strike
It'll be your turn, high and mighty gentlemen
To climb onto the plateau
And if it's war that you want
Then pay for it with your own skin

WORLD WAR ONE

An Illustrated Chronology

Jean-Pierre
VERNEY

All photographs courtesy
of the MUSÉE DE LA
GRANDE GUERRE
DU PAYS DE MEAUX

A German family.

1914

A French family.

Paris, June 28, 1914. Under a bright afternoon sun, Raymond Poincaré, President of the French Republic, was watching the running of the Grand Prix at the Longchamp race track.

That is where a messenger dispatched from the Ministry of Foreign Affairs discreetly informed him of the assassination of Archduke Franz Ferdi-nand, heir to the Austro-Hungarian throne, and his wife, in the little Bosnian town of Sarajevo.

"The Allies fly to victory."

At the time, the event went almost unnoticed. Certainly nobody imagined it would lead virtually all of the great Western powers to yield to the siren song of wartime adventure.

Who, upon hearing the news, could have predicted that European civilization was about to buckle under the weight of national rivalries and prostrate itself before the implacable machinery of military alliances?

Who could have anticipated the onset of war fever, or the escalating madness of the days to come, as the press whipped up public sentiment?

Why would anyone have doubted the diplomats? Surely they were sensible enough to persuade the heads of state to ignore the pressure leveled at them by the generals, blinded by their strategic plans?

A patriotic German postcard: "When you cheerfully return from battle and strife / The young girls rush to your side."

Of course, these officers had been preparing for a major confrontation for years—that was their job. But the responsibility for declaring war belonged to others.

In 1914, Europe was a beacon of civilization to the world, unchallenged in its influence, and seemingly with nothing to fear. Nothing, that is, except itself.

A left-wing coalition had just won the general election in France. The controversy over a recently passed new law extending compulsory military service to three years had dominated the campaign, along with a plan to introduce the income tax and the issue of secular education.

However, as early as June 19, the new Chamber of Deputies approved an 800-million-franc armament loan. East of the Rhine, a squadron of British ships had recently paid a friendly visit to Kiel, Germany's chief naval port. Blood ties connected the royal houses of many European nations: Czar Nicholas II of Russia, King George V of England, and Kaiser Wilhelm II of Germany were all cousins through the deceased Queen Victoria.

And yet Europe was, in 1914, deeply divided between two distinct and antagonistic groups. On the one side, there were the Central Powers of Germany, Austria-Hungary, and Italy, aligned through the Triple Alliance; on the other, the Allied Powers or Triple Entente of France, Russia, and England.

Unsurprisingly, the situation exposed conflicting interests and stoked rivalries, trade disputes, chauvinism, and colonial antagonism. Occasionally, it resulted in tensions and even led to talk of war, but so far, crises had always been averted through diplomacy.

Letter to readers of Gil Blas from the publishers announcing the magazine's suspension as the entire staff has joined the army.

It is true that France and Germany had been engaged in an arms race for the past 30 years. This subtle but perilous game of chicken had pushed each nation to keep building up its weapons and troops to levels at least matching those of its potential opponent.

It is true that the extremely rapid development of Germany's naval strength

German postcard celebrating the upcoming "great victory."

worried and antagonized Britain, which was bent on remaining the unrivaled master of the seas.

It is true that the Balkan nations on the borders of Eastern Europe had recently suffered through two wars, with the significant outcome that Turkey had lost nearly all its possessions in the region. While European diplomats played an active role in negotiating treaties to establish the new borders, they were unable to spare Bulgaria

The socialist magazines fall in line with the war effort: "National Defense Comes First! They Assassinated Jaurès; We Will Not Assassinate France."

of the proletariat and the General Confederation of Labor (CGT). Waging war

Civilian population fleeing ahead of the German invasion.

So what was there to worry about, then?

The dog days of July came and went. In Vienna, the royal couple was given a discreet funeral and the guilty were put under lock and key. In Germany, the Kaiser declared his unconditional loyalty to the elderly Emperor Franz Joseph on the eve of his 84th birthday, and then left on a cruise.

There was nothing to suggest that relations between the Austro-Hungarian Empire and the small kingdom of Serbia would fray. The sensational assassination was already no more than a distant and minor disturbance. But a few players had begun to gamble behind the scenes, enlisting the destinies of millions of men as their tokens.

On July 23, Austria presented Serbia with a brutal and humiliating ultimatum. European diplomats tried to intervene, but the nails of strife had already been driven too deep into the cross upon which the world was about to crucify itself. On July 25, the Russian Czar, fresh from hosting a visit by the French President Poincaré, declared his support for Serbia. And on July 28, Austria, buttressed by Kaiser Wilhelm II's support, declared war on Serbia and thereby threw open the great ball to its inaugural dance.

The mobilization waltz could now begin. Blow the horns, roll the drums: the opening notes had sounded for all, but accompanied with the firm belief that it would end swiftly—"before the first leaves fall."

"In the Trenches"

Beginning on July 30, more than 10 million men were called to report to duty. Some answered with enthusiasm, others with curses, and most out of a sense of duty. In France, the assassination of Jaurès notwithstanding, political divisions were paved over by the "Sacred Union," a truce declared between left and right in the face of the enemy. So much for the Workers International and its faith in pacifist action.

the ignominy of emerging as the other major loser, its territorial claims having been refused in favor of Greece's.

French regiment marching toward the front.

against war through general strikes and potentially through revolt: to both the French and the German working classes, this was the panacea that could stand up against the bourgeoisie, the arms merchants, and war-mongers in general.

But it is also true that millions of Europeans had, over the past decade or so, rallied around the pacifist resolutions of the powerful Workers International and looked to socialism as a guarantor of peace. In France, Jean Jaurès, a Socialist deputy and a true "voice of the people," helped set the agenda of the Workers International. Though he recognized national defense as a duty as well as the necessity of the preservation of national independence, he carried high the hopes

August 1914: French infantrymen awaiting the enemy.

September 1914: French troops during the Battle of the Marne.

France's strategy was almost exclusively offensive. The infantry was "the queen of battle"—versatile and decisive, like its chess counterpart. The shining bayonet was its torch and the 75 mm field gun its metronome. One can only wonder in retrospect at the apparent disregard for the "killing fire" of machine guns and heavy artillery.

Joffre attacked in Alsace and kept an eye on the enemy in Lorraine, eager to even the score in these territories lost to Germany in the Franco-Prussian war of 1870-71. But Germany advanced via Belgium. This violation of

German infantrymen.

On August 2, with crops in the fields and a promising grape harvest in sight, workers, employers, peasants, bourgeois, and businessmen, all gathered together by law, began trading in their civilian clothes for uniforms, before being summoned to take on their longstanding enemies. Battle would be engaged according to top-secret plans, carefully devised over decades by generals convinced of their own brilliance and proud of their tactical skills.

In Paris, intoxicated by the declaration of war, frenzied mobs attacked "German" businesses. Cafés and shops were looted merely because they had German-sounding names. A number of grocery stores shared this fate, including those in the Maggi chain, although it was in fact headquartered in Switzerland.

It had enjoyed a fine reputation, too, especially for its natural products, its pure milk, and its commitment to providing nutritional and affordable food for working-class families. But now the "Bouillon Kub," a brand of stock cubes produced by Maggi, provoked popular fury. For months, a press campaign orchestrated by the extreme right and its vocal proponent

Léon Daudet had insidiously suggested that "Maggi" and "Kub" were fronts for German spy activity, and that the thousands of Kub billboards posted throughout the countryside were actually signposts indicating military objectives for invading troops. Concern was so great that on August 4, the French Minister of the Interior ordered the destruction of the those posters displayed near military zones and rail lines.

Thousands of trains ran along those rail lines, one after the other, each with its heavy cargo of young men. Like a well-oiled machine, they carried the nation's future to its borders. In the dank, foul air of the cattle cars, a few recruits still had the strength to sing *La Chanson du départ* (The Song of the Departure): "Victory singing opens the gate for us / Liberty guides our steps / And from the north to the south the trumpet of war / Has sounded the hour of combat."

French infantrymen.

Belgian neutrality brought Britain into the war—a turn of events that took Germany by surprise. Meanwhile, Joffre's offensive forays in Alsace and Lorraine proved short-lived. By August 25, with pressure on all his armies, Joffre ordered a general retreat.

Joffre's predictions had all been proven wrong. But more importantly, the amount of French casualties was becoming terrifying, on some days exceeding 25,000 dead.

In Paris, headlines jubilantly announced that the Russians were only a five-day march from Berlin. Yet the next day, the papers jolted their readers with news that the Germans had arrived at the gates of Paris.

On September 2, in order to provide new impetus to

the national defense effort, the government withdrew to Bordeaux and appointed Joseph Gallieni, a retired general, to defend the capital. Joffre, however, had little regard for Gallieni and would repeatedly remind him who was in charge.

When the German armies had advanced to less than 15 miles outside of Paris, they undertook an imprudent maneuver. Convinced that the French units had been defeated and that the remnants of the British Expeditionary Force were trying only to reach the coast and their ships, the German generals decided to step up the pace and annihilate the exposed Allied forces in the open countryside. Rather than encircle the capital as planned, they chose to flank Paris from the north.

Quick to recognize this change of direction as an unexpected stroke of luck,

German wounded.

Gallieni decided to launch an attack on this exposed flank.

With some effort, he convinced Joffre to seize the opportunity, in an operation that would become known as the Battle of the Marne.

On September 6, some 800,000 French and 60,000

And yet these tens of thousands of men—after retreating for almost two weeks, short on provisions, in suffocating heat, sweating beneath the weight of some 55 lbs. of "piss-poor" equipment and a uniform that was too warm for the season—pulled themselves together and turned back toward the front.

Many more would fall in the shade of the ear-laden cornstalks.

In another Gallieni initiative, some 2,000 infantrymen were placed into several hundred commandeered taxis to join the battle at Nanteuil-le-Haudouin.

These reinforcements comprised just a drop in the bucket of this massive confrontation, but they helped steal victory from the brilliant German General Alexander Von Kluck, who had hoped to strike a decisive blow. The taxis drove into history books, the stuff of modern legend.

Joffre. Gallieni was ignored. The censor's hand was busy and it had selected its hero.

All the newspapers paid tribute to the bravery of the British professional army. They also extolled the incredible pluck displayed by Belgium's ill-equipped troops, celebrated the courage of its people, and praised its king. But balancing the good news came reports from the eastern front that two Russian armies, while pushing into East Prussia, had been annihilated at Tannenberg and on the shores of the Masurian lakes by Paul von Hindenburg, a seasoned German general recalled from retirement.

The press also noted the difficulties arising from the massive arrival of tens of thousands of refugees fleeing from the invaders. But looming above all were reports of gratuitous violence perpetrated by the

gruesome physical wounds, and equally horrifying psychological ones as well.

People saw that many who hoped to recover instead died unimaginable deaths from gas gangrene that spread in infected wounds. Evacuated troops traveled for hours and sometimes days in "8-horse, 40-man" rail cars, sleeping in straw soiled by horse manure. Nobody thought to clean out the cars and change the bedding.

With most of the men away, women, children, and the elderly now shouldered the heavy burden of keeping the economy running. They had to feed the armies, exchange torn and worn items, replace lost rifles, and supply the cannons with firepower.

The 75 mm field gun was the pride of the French artillery, though it was shorter in reach than German heavy artillery, and desperately in need of shells.

French trench.

German trench.

British soldiers engaged 800,000 Germans in a brutal struggle along a line extending from Verdun to the Oise. The battles were savage, confused, but always deadly. Outside Meaux, the beloved French poet Charles Péguy died under enemy fire—a death he had aspired to and glorified in verse: "Happy are those who die for the carnal earth / provided the war is just." A short distance away, five soldiers, no worse than the rest but who had turned back out of hunger, racked by diarrhea and cramps from eating unripe fruit along the way, were summarily shot by a general: executed to set an example.

After a brief retreat, the Germans regrouped and, using the terrain, dug in from Verdun to the Oise, in advantageous and easily-defended positions.

A network of continuous trenches began to take shape. Attempting to outflank each other, the two enemies battled their way up to the North Sea. No longer did anyone believe in "a short and glorious war," in lightning cavalry attacks with drawn swords, or in being home by Christmas.

The civilian population had been deluged with accounts of the brilliant victory of the Marne and the man behind it, General

German armies. Lootings, ransoms, rapes, crimes, hostage-takings, and the destruction of monuments and churches were luridly described in the papers. No detail was omitted in stories about wounded soldiers left to die, children gunned down, and priests tortured by the "Huns," the "barbarians," the "Vandals." Sadly absent was any news about France's own, however.

People knew there had been prisoners, casualties, and fatalities. Day by day, trains rolled into stations across the country, bringing back victims in the hundreds. Hospitals had to be opened and staff found to manage

But since the war had been expected to last only six to eight weeks, adequate production had not been planned. And with the workers on the front, the factories were empty. Quick solutions were needed to address the labor, steel, and tool shortages. Above all, the demand for gunpowder and explosives had to be filled. But it was Germany, Europe's industrial powerhouse, that was the main supplier of the chemicals used by France's explosives factories. The crisis became so acute that by late 1914, Joffre made daily tallies of the number of shells available per cannon. And this situation persisted

into 1915, with tragic consequences.

For the time being, combat gradually moved away from the Paris area but remained violent and deadly.

The Germans, like the French, were out for nothing less than total annihilation of the adversary. To satisfy the pressing needs of battle, tens of thousands of men were moved from east to west, but without notable success. And soon the lines approached the Belgian border.

and the men's greatcoats were in tatters.

To respond to the situation, the Parisian fashion designer Paul Poiret was called on to design a new coat. Easier to wear (it had a turned-down collar), quicker to assemble and sew (the seams were streamlined), and economical (it required less fabric and fewer buttons), it was also cut from cloth of a new color: "horizon blue." But it remained a far cry from the

But the small British army continued to fight alongside its French and Belgian "brothers in arms."

And day by day, the war crawled on.

Daily official reports brought news of struggles in the Yser plain. To halt the German advance, Belgium had opened the canal locks controlling tidal flows, and soon the region was transformed into an immense lake in which men slogged, animals drowned, and cannons became mired. And in the midst of it all, the battles intensified.

The German side greeted hordes of young students who had enlisted enthusiastically in August. With only brief training, they were wastefully sacrificed in attack after attack. To this day, Germany remembers the First Battle of Ypres as the "Massacre of the Innocents."

On the French side, the feats of the marine fusiliers became legendary, while the North African and Black African troops engaged in the sector suffered unimaginable losses.

Finally, in early December, the last skirmishes on the shores of the North Sea took place, resulting in a draw of sorts.

The two sides were now entrenched along some 500 miles of front. The troops were exhausted, munitions were rationed, and the losses were staggering.

Eleven French departments, including some

of the country's richest administrative divisions, began their new lives under German occupation, and the population was dismayed at the many harsh measures imposed by the "Kommandantur."

Even more devastating, the great industrial power of France's coal and iron mines, textile mills, and blast furnaces was now in the service of the Reich's wartime economy.

Germany would be able to continue its offensive.

Christmas was right around the corner. The American president Woodrow Wilson sent offers from Washington to mediate, and in Rome, Pope Benedict XV proposed a Christmas truce. The suggestion was swiftly rejected by all the governments, but the idea filtered down to the trenches, where German and British troops in particular dared to celebrate Christmas together in unofficial ceasefires.

But their good will did nothing to thwart the momentum of the deadly violence and meant nothing to the vast numbers of individuals permanently fallen, having died for "Fatherland," "King," "Emperor," and even "God."

❖

December 1914: Wounded soldiers by the hundreds of thousands.

Fall came, and a wintry chill was already in the air. The soldiers, suffering war fatigue and endlessly tested by their traumatic living conditions, now had to endure cold and rain. Needless to say, no plans had been made for winter warfare. Tarps were rare, blankets were obtained by pillaging homes,

elegance and quality of the uniforms used by British troops.

Indeed, the British officers were often shocked, to say the least, by the low birth of many of the French generals, simple citizens without crests or other marks of nobility to distinguish them.

1914 by the Numbers

350,000 Frenchmen, 250,000 Germans,
20,000 Englishmen, 15,000 Belgians, and 200,000 Russians
dead within five months, not to mention Serbs, Austrians,
Hungarians, Turks, and Japanese.

The Battle of the Marne — September 5 – 13.

On the French side: 21,000 dead,
122,000 wounded, 84,000 missing.
On the British side: 3,000 dead,
30,000 wounded, 4,000 missing.
On the German side: 43,000 dead,
173,000 wounded, 40,000 missing.

On the French front.

1915

On the German front.

Winter had set in. The illusions and assumptions of July 1914—the kind so often shared by nations entering into war—had been disproven. Shattered, too, were the plans and doctrines of the general staffs, developed over years and intended to ensure victory in just a few weeks.

From the North Sea to the Swiss border, the soldiers were now dug in for the long haul. They needed to face this fact and adapt to the new realities of trench life, and to trench warfare as well.

Germany's new Chief of the General Staff, General Erich von Falkenhayn, planned to remain on the defensive on the French front in order to focus on defeating Russia's armies in the east. The French and the British, meanwhile, had no intention of giving up the initiative.

The British, believing a breakthrough on the western front to be impossible, sought a new theater of operations and found it in Asia Minor. Eliminating Turkey would limit the naval threat in the Mediterranean, intensify the encirclement of Austria-Hungary and Germany, relieve the Russian front, and facilitate liaison with Russia. They therefore made plans to force open the Dardanelles Straits, a strategically valuable connection between the Mediterranean and the Black Seas.

A first naval operation, carried out in February, ended in failure. In March, a second attempt launched from the powerful British and French fleets was no more successful: within hours, one French and two British battleships had been sunk and four others dam-

In a French trench.

aged. This new upset led the Allies to attempt an amphibious attack on the Gallipoli peninsula, at the southern tip of the Dardanelles. On April 25, French, British, Australian, and New Zealand forces landed along the beaches but remained contained on the coast, unable to advance.

Although reinforcements were sent, Turkish troops, led by a German general, cut off all Allied attempts at progress toward the interior.

With the Turks holding the high ground, the Allied soldiers found themselves in a particularly grim situation. The challenges of fighting in hostile terrain, compounded by illness, supply problems, and the proliferation of rats and flies, contributed to the deaths of more than 160,000 men, including 30,000 French **troops.**

The campaign ended in unmitigated failure. In late 1915, as Germany and Austria defeated the Serbs with the help of Bulgaria (which had just joined the Central Powers), the Allies pulled out of the Dardanelles, transferring some of their divisions to Salonika, Greece.

By early January, 1916, there were no Allied soldiers left in the Dardanelles. A new front had opened up in the Balkans, however, with the Allied *Armée d'Orient* ("Army of the Orient") under French command.

Meanwhile, General Joffre, obstinate by nature, but hailed as a hero by the press and considered a virtual savior by the public since the "Miracle of the Marne," refused to accept a static strategy. He remained convinced that initiative was needed to break the German lines and push back the enemy. Accordingly, he persisted with offensive actions throughout the year. Was he blind to the obvious superiority of Germany's heavy artillery, which was being used in support of an intelligent defensive strategy? Was he not aware of how weary his men were? Had he failed to analyze the actual reasons for shell shortages, or realized how

Allied troops in Gallipoli (Turkey).

A French machine gun on the Serbian front.

French artillery.

Spring 1915: The new French uniform.

Besides, as he openly stated, he believed the war would be over before a helmet could be made. A quartermaster, August-Louis Adrian, proposed provisional protection in the form of a rudimentary skull-cap, the *cervelière* ("brain pan"). Rapidly manufactured and distributed, it wasn't popular with the troops, but its use led to a clear decrease in the incidence and severity of head injuries.

With the war continuing, Adrian created a more comfortable and practical steel cap that was also designed to be cheap and easy to manufacture.

When the new model was finally approved, it went into large-scale production, and by the end of the year, 3 million helmets had been delivered to the army.

fragile the manufacturing sector had become?

It was not until midway through the year that first steps were taken to establish a war economy and implement munitions production.

tively limited or neutralized all offensive action?

Did he give any thought to the everyday reality of the troops? Those poor wretches, holed up in their dugouts, dressed in rags, foul-smelling,

France's lack of industrial preparation was also evident in its rifle shortage. By early 1915, 450,000 Lebel rifles, representing one sixth of all available arms, had already been exhausted.

Behind French lines.

Behind German lines.

Had Joffre fully assessed the heavy price of *attaque à outrance* ("attack to excess"), France's aggressive doctrine of the offensive?

Did he realize that the Germans' defensive measures, perfected daily, effec-

filthy, bone-cold and poorly equipped, could only wonder if the war would ever end.

The soldiers of the winter of 1914-1915 mostly looked and lived like scavengers. In the months to come, however, they would be outfitted with new uniforms, dyed the pale blue-gray that came to be known as "horizon blue." The first steel helmets were distributed in July, and their silhouette would enter the history books as a defining symbol of the French soldiers of World War I.

And yet the introduction of those helmets had been a struggle in itself.

With the advent of trench warfare, head wounds had quickly become commonplace. Although protection was obviously necessary, Joffre preferred to allocate steel to shell production.

German trenches in the dunes of the North Sea.

Rifle production had been suspended a decade earlier, and no plans had been made for the event of mobilization. The Ministry of War attempted to negotiate deals, especially abroad, but with limited results. Although unsatisfactory for the front-line troops, one makeshift solution was the retooling of 700,000 single-shot Gras model 74 rifles for use with the 8 mm cartridges of the Lebel rifle.

In January, 40,000 refitted Gras rifles were delivered to the troops. But another half year passed before the development of a new rifle got underway, with the support of private manufacturers: it was the 07/15, based on a weapon originally distributed to France's colonial troops and equipped with a three-shot magazine.

High command had, however, been studying and testing light machine guns since the turn of the century, and it now decided to strengthen the infantry's firepower. A hurried deci-

sion was made to manufacture a machine gun based on a prototype tested in 1910, which was supposed to be suitable for mass production: the Chau-chat 1915 light machine gun. After a difficult start, production rose to more than 13,500 units a month in October 1915. Though much maligned, this weapon prefigured the mass-produced, low-cost automatic weapons of WWII.

Joffre, who had gradually assumed the role of de facto commander of the Allied armies, remained certain that a breakthrough could be achieved. Without waiting, he launched several successive attempts to crack the western front, each more powerful and more lethal than the last.

Joffre's offensive campaign began in Champagne in early 1915, where 90,000 men supported by 200 old cannons barely managed to scratch the German lines. It continued, uselessly, in the Aisne.

In spring, the French General HQ (GQG) ordered a series of assaults on the Artois front. Joffre optimistically declared to the President of France, Raymond Poincaré, "I expect to obtain a resolution in France before the month of May." There were of course a few local success-

es, but the cost was staggering. Finally, in fall, Joffre launched his "victory offensive." In all, 300,000 men supported by 2,000 cannons attacked Champagne on a front barely 20 miles long, and 100,000 others launched a fresh attack on the already bloodied soil of Artois. A few advances were made and a few crests scaled, a few woods crossed, and a few front lines taken. A few men even managed to get behind

German lines in the chalklands of Champagne, but they had to stop, exhausted, and reinforcements never arrived.

Though a few miles were gained, the graves multiplying along the line of fire testified to the cost. The public,

meanwhile, was unaware of this proliferation of crosses, lulled and brainwashed as it was by the controlled press. Censorship prohibited criticism of the government, the army, its leaders, or the general conduct of the war. Instead, newspaper readers were inundated with reports about the cooperation and achievements of the Allied troops, the success of the maritime blockade, and the resulting famine in the Central Empires. Propaganda campaigns also focused attention on the poor quality of German munitions, condemned the cowardice of the "Boches," and exaggerated their losses. With such reporting to go by, the public could hardly begin

September 1915: In Champagne, the French troops rejoin the front lines.

nades and small-arms fire to which they were subjected.

One French response was the homemade grenade, made of a wad of guncotton, a length of fuse, and a bottle or tin can packed with gravel, nails, and shrapnel. There was of course the regulation bracelet grenade, dating back to the First Empire, but since it was generally reserved for the defense of forts, very few reached the trenches. And so soldiers quickly responded by using available material, pieces of wood, and explosive charges to make crude petard and stick grenades.

New models and designs were being developed on all sides, both inside and outside the military, in France and abroad. Dozens of devices were tested and dozens more purchased, but it would be the end of the year before soldiers received safe and effective regulation models.

The underground war.

to appreciate the realities of the war. The soldiers themselves, whether to reassure loved ones or out of discretion, withheld information about the daily horrors they were experiencing.

If a kind of stubborn folly and profound lack of imagination characterized the major assaults of 1915, the same can certainly be said of the smaller local operations launched on German positions over the course of the year. Often initiated by high command to maintain troop morale and destabilize the enemy, they mostly missed the mark, considering the results achieved and the costs and losses incurred.

Argonne, Woëvre, Vauquois, Vosges, Éparges, Linge, Vieil-Armand: these and other sectors all saw furious and deadly mêlées, fought between a few hundred soldiers for days and sometimes weeks at a time. The gains were sparse: a few meters of ground, a mine crater, a lookout post, the charred remains of a forest or a devastated village.

While the French lines were not always advantageously drawn and could certainly have benefited from adjustment, the loss of tens of thousands of lives

in the process reflected nothing so much as obstinacy back at general headquarters, which remained unable to adapt to this static war. Worse yet, the losses were so disastrous that they became grounds for new skirmishes: it was necessary to prove that previous sacrifices had not been in vain.

The "war of the moles" required specific weapons,

materials, and protective devices in a time of general shortages. While waiting for industry to provide trench artillery, grenades, armored shields, corrugated iron for shelters, and barbed wire, French troops improvised simple but effective devices to respond to the firepower of the many mortars installed in the German front lines, as well as the hail of hand gre-

September 1915: German prisoners of war.

Artillerymen also had to resort to improvisation. Although a few century-old mortars had been hauled out of the arsenals, they could hardly compensate for France's inferior firepower. And so the Cellerier mortar was invented—a make-shift mortar tube made from the case of a German 77 or 105 mm shell and loaded with an artillery cartridge. Rudimentary and easy to make and use, these little trench mortars comprised France's only response to Germany's powerful Minen-werfer in the fall and winter of 1914-1915.

It was a soldier who eventually interceded with Joffre to obtain the means to test and manufacture France's first real trench mortar, the 58 mm. Though hastily developed and crudely constructed (it consisted of a simple barrel over which was fitted the short tail of a large finned shell), it quickly took its place on the front lines.

Once adopted, it was rapidly improved and delivered in the hundreds, capable of launching ever-heavier and more destructive torpedoes over a distance of some 200 to 300 yards. The popular mortar was nicknamed the *crapouillot*—"little toad." Typically operated by the more reckless soldiers, its arrival in the front lines was not always welcomed by infantry. Indeed, its presence often signaled the need for extra support or preparation for an attack, and its firing immediately elicited and provided a target for dangerous and much feared German retorts.

The Germans adapted best to the nerve-wracking stalemate. Yet despite the German army's superior firepower, defensive strategy, tradition of combat engineers, and early recognition that entrenchment would lead to drawn-out engagement, it too had to resort to the use of improvised mortars and ammunition throughout 1915.

To break the deadlock of trench warfare, Germany, recognized as Europe's leading industrial power and chemical producer, turned to quick yet brutal methods. In so doing, it took on the fraught responsibility for introducing the use of poison gas, drawing on pre-war research by a scientific section of the War Office in Berlin dedicated to the military application of scientific and industrial innovations.

Under the supervision of the world-renowned chemist Fritz Haber, one focus of the studies was the use of asphyxiating gases to immobilize enemy troops.

This project was in clear violation of the 1889 Hague Conventions prohibiting the use of chemical weapons and burning liquids. In 1914 and early 1915, tests were carried out in France and on the eastern front, but cold weather hampered the vaporization of the gases and limited their effects: The exposed soldiers were merely indisposed. The decision was then made to introduce the technique on the western front over a larger area.

In early April, in the Ypres sector in Belgium, a German deserter reported that the enemy was preparing a powerful offensive that would be preceded by a release of toxic gas. Despite the detailed explanation, the information was not taken seriously and no warning or recommendation was passed on to the troops.

In the late afternoon of April 22, French, Belgian, British, and Canadian infantry watched, curious, as a yellow-green fog rose from the German trenches. Carried by a light wind, this first major release of what was in fact chlorine gas killed more than 5,000 troops. But the Germans were unable to benefit from the element of surprise and their new weapon, rather than bringing the conflict to an end, only added to the torment that all soldiers had to endure.

Quickly, each side undertook to increase the toxicity of the gases used, refine their means of dispersal, and provide soldiers with individual protective devices. The first of these were simple cotton pads issued with goggles, but they gave way to hoods and eventually to more sophisticated masks with filter canisters.

Around the same time, also in violation of the Hague Conventions, Germans in Argonne introduced the use of inflammable liquids, projected by flamethrowers. Though these new weapons did not revolutionize the war, they contributed to its cruelty and inhumanity.

Meanwhile, a hill in the same region, the Butte de Vauquois, topped by a small Lorraine village, became synonymous with another form of attack: mine warfare. This ancient method of siege warfare continued underground for months. German combat engineers and French sappers engaged in anxious subterranean battles, digging hundreds of meters' worth of tunnels and filling chambers with tons of explosive charges.

Atop the hill, the powerless infantry could only hope to be relieved before an explosion occurred. The village was pulverized, the summit of the hill was pockmarked by ever-deeper craters, and dozens of men disappeared, buried and crushed. What could possibly justify this agonizing form of warfare? Obliterating a few dozen or even 100 square meters of ground: what more could it achieve than the brutal destruction of a few more lives?

In the face of so much misery, anguish, and suffering, soldiers could do little except wait for it to end. For some, the trial was so great that they sought relief through self-harm or suicide. Others tried to distance themselves from the hell of war by inducing symptoms, wounds or illnesses in desperate attempts to gain evacuation. Some physicians took undistinguished pleasure in accusing genuinely (or falsely) injured men of self-inflicted wounds—an offense for which the penalty was execution by firing squad. Military justice was swift and merciless. Above all, it aimed to set an example: there was no forgiving mutiny and desertion.

Especially severe and troubling was the practice of decimation. In a few instances, men were arbitrarily selected for execution to answer for a company or battalion's failure to carry out orders, reasonable or not. Some officers misused the military courts, injustices were committed, and terrible mistakes were made. All in the name of discipline.

A few soldiers, though not many, chose to desert or sur-

The same year also saw the appearance of an unusual kind of publication: the "soldier newspaper." Ribald, moving, and mostly short-lived, these little trench publications were quick to find humor in everything, written as they were by men who couldn't know what the next day would bring. Varying in professionalism, erratically published, they caused considerable concern at army headquarters. Ultimately, though, this "blue horizon" press was officially condoned as a morale booster.

May brought another important decision, one that had been eagerly awaited and would be much appre-

Fall 1915: Behind the British lines.

September 1915: After an assault, French infantrymen wearing the Adrian helmet.

ciated by the soldiers as well as their families: the granting of furlough. Five days of leave, transportation time included, could never be long enough, of course. But coming back home to family, children, and friends, scrubbing off the dirt of the trenches, taking a stroll without risking one's life: these were precious moments, stolen away from the slaughter and the hell.

Police officials and mayors continued to deliver death notices to families. As a mark of supreme tribute, the French government instituted the *Croix de guerre* ("cross of war"), a military decoration awarded to sol-

diers who had distinguished themselves through bravery. And in July, it was stipulated that the mention *Mort pour la France* ("Died for France") would be entered in the Registry of Civil Status alongside the names of all soldiers and civilians killed by the enemy.

The soldiers in the trenches continued to acquiesce to the circumstances. A development in May seemed to offer encouragement: Italy, after weeks of negotiation and sordid dealings, had entered the war on the side of the Allies and declared war on Austria. But soon this new European front was simply another mass grave.

render to the enemy. Joffre informed the troops that all returned prisoners would be tried at war's end.

Meanwhile, day-to-day life on the front line was Hell. Death hovered everywhere. Even maintaining basic hygiene was an impossible task. Backbreaking tasks kept the troops busy day and night. The trenches were dirty, muddy, and foul smelling, but since the French side still clung to the belief that it was all provisional, nothing was done to rectify the situation. Lack of privacy, homesickness, and the shortage of news, especially for men from regions now under occupation, caused discouragement and depression.

Some kept their minds busy through manual activity. The year 1915, in particular, saw the production across the entire front of utilitarian and artistic objects, soon known as trench art.

A makeshift workshop for the creation of trench art.

Death as an everyday event.

The war continued, with no end in sight. Short on firepower, Joffre stripped the forts of their weapons and reassembled old Bange system cannons in the most dangerous sectors. At best, they could fire shells every three or four minutes. Meanwhile, the field artillery faced a major crisis. The new 75 shells had been too rapidly manufactured—they were turned, not forged—and they would burst in the cannon barrels on firing. Artillerymen

On the German front.

were killed and injured as a result, and hundreds of 75 mm field guns were rendered useless.

And still the war continued. On the Russian front, the Germans and the Austrians forced the Czar's troops to retreat some 100 miles, but they could not annihilate them, despite the considerable numbers thrown into their pursuit.

In the fall, war fever gripped Bulgaria as well,

and it joined forces with Austria-Hungary and Germany to invade Serbia. Attacked from the north and the east, the Serbian army could do little but retreat toward the Adriatic coast. French reinforcements from Salonika arrived too late to provide assistance. Though Joffre, who wanted to keep all forces on his own front, looked upon the *Armée d'Orient* with disdain, the unit would go on to make its mark later in the war.

In the Middle East, Russia and Turkey continued to face one another on the Caucasus front. Further south, an Ottoman army attempting to cross the Suez Canal was driven off by the British defenders, who brought in a steady stream of reinforcements, mostly from the East Indies, Australia, and New Zealand. But a new tragedy had begun: the deportation of the Armenian population.

In the Mesopotamian desert, British troops moving toward Baghdad were forced to turn back and surrender to the Turks. It was a considerable humiliation, and it tarnished the reputation of the British Empire in the eyes of Arab populations. In Africa, meanwhile, almost all German possessions passed into Allied hands.

And the war continued on. In December, Joffre was appointed Commander in Chief of the French armies. Questioned about his military actions, he stated that he was "nibbling" at the Germans. Did he not

know how many men had died since January? In 1915, France added a further 350,000 fallen troops to the number of those already killed in 1914.

But for the time being, Joffre's main concern was the gathering of all heads of the Allied armies at his Chantilly headquarters. It was already time to plan the major offensives for 1916. The decision: attack on all fronts, in the east, in the south, in the west.

Meanwhile, the German high command had decided to shift the focus of its efforts to the western front: France was the enemy to be beaten, and Verdun the strategic objective.

December 1916: The Allied commanders at the General Headquarters in Chantilly.

1915 by the Numbers
French soldiers killed, missing, or taken prisoner:

December 1914 and January 1915: 74,000.
February and March: 69,000.
April through June: 142,000.
July and August: 48,000.
September through November: 131,000.
Total: 464,000.

Total number of soldiers wounded during 1915: 1,326,911.
Total number of soldiers reported ill: 1,177,390.
Total number of soldiers discharged to pension (January 1, 1916): 278,000.

The Battle of Champagne
from September 25 to October 15, 1915
Killed, missing, taken prisoner: 81,509.
Wounded: 98,305.

1916

Misinformed by general headquarters and sidelined by Joffre, the French government had been effectively excluded from military decision making since August 1914. But as questions and grievances piled up, it began to reassert itself.

Command deficiencies, the notorious material shortages, diplomatic missteps, and the general conduct of the war were some of the issues being raised and debated in parliament. Hoping to revive national unity and quell growing concerns and criticism, the prime minister, Aristide Briand, appointed Joffre as commander-in-chief of the French Army on December

2, 1915. The promotion suited Joffre's ambitions. He believed the Allied armies needed a leader, and the new appointment brought him a step closer to this position.

A field kitchen.

And so it was a confident Joffre who convened the key Allied commanders at his headquarters in the Château de Chantilly on December 6. His proposal for coordinated offensives on all Allied fronts was unanimously accepted, with early summer chosen as the best time to attack.

The success of this major inter-allied conference demonstrated that its participants be willing to grant Joffre a certain power of command. Though not designated as such, he was considered the head of the Allied armies. However, General Haig, commander of the British forces, also had ambitions to lead operations on the western front.

January 1916: Fort Douaumont.

Consistent with Joffre's agenda, a plan for a joint offensive on the western front was adopted in early February. The battle would be led by General Foch, commanding the Northern Army Group, and the attack would be carried out in the Somme area by 42 divisions, supported by 1,700 heavy guns. The British nevertheless mounted their own operation independently, to the detriment of the massive attack approved at Chantilly.

The Germans, meanwhile, were feeling the effects of the Allied naval blockade. Having failed to achieve the victory they had expected on the Russian front, they now urgently sought to avoid a

further prolongation of the war. A major military victory over France or Great Britain, they believed, would force negotiations. And given the circumstances, such a settlement would favor Germany, just as it had at the end of the Franco-Prussian War.

General Erich von Falkenhayn, the chief of the German General Staff, strategized accordingly. Held in check throughout 1915 by the exasperating elasticity of the Russian front, he now decided to shift his forces abruptly to the western front and focus his efforts there.

Absorbed by preparations for his own offensive, Joffre dismissed the warnings that reached Chantilly in early January 1916. And yet increasingly specific tips and intelligence indicated that the Germans were planning an assault north of Verdun in early February.

The rumors reached parliament and the president as well. Concerned, Poincaré informed Joffre that he intended to tour the fortified region of Verdun as soon as possible to assess the situation firsthand. Joffre detained him by offering to go along. And Poincaré

The calm before the German attack.

February 21: The German offensive.

its 28 forts and outposts, some of which were recently built, it remained a key pillar of the French front line. Fort Douaumont, a massive earthen shield set before the city, was considered its unassailable guardian.

However, the French front in this sector formed a large salient jutting dangerously into German lines, exposing the French forces to German artillery fire on two sides.

Moreover, this protrusion of French-controlled land was

persuaded the Kaiser that a brutal military defeat of the historic town would deal a severe blow to French public and troop morale. It would also restore the prestige of the German army, presenting a serious obstacle to preparations for the great Franco-British attack expected in the coming months. The element of surprise would be crucial. The operation would be concentrated on a very narrow stretch of front, limiting the

agreed, as he had an urgent matter that he wished to discuss with Joffre in Verdun. Poincaré had heard from various sources that the area's defenses were in poor repair. For several weeks now, Driant, an army officer, but also a writer and a representative to the Chamber of Deputies, had been raising alarm about the absence of a second line and about re-supply and reinforcement difficulties. A number of generals, troubled by decisions made at general headquarters, had not hesitated to pass on details to sympathetic parliamentarians.

Still Joffre remained silent. Poincaré persisted and took his concerns to Joseph Gallieni, the new Minister of War. Under increasing pressure, Joffre at last offered assurances and justifications. But he was outraged by the challenge to his authority and demanded to know the names of his detractors. He made it clear that he would brook no criticism: "The very fact that the government welcomes communications of this kind… deeply disturbs the spirit of discipline in the Army."

Nonetheless, he did send General de Castelnau to inspect the region on January 19. The general

returned with a harsh, even alarmist, report on defensive vulnerabilities in the sector. Joffre, entirely focused on his action plan for the battle at the Somme, remained unconvinced. He considered that "strategically, seen from the German side, a battle for Verdun does not justify itself. […] The end of the war can only be achieved through a major upset, and this terrain is not conducive to such a turn of events." It was not until February 10 that he

February 23: French prisoners.

February 25: French reinforcements arrive.

acknowledged the possibility of a major German attack on Verdun. From Chantilly, he gave orders for preparations to direct war material, cannons (a total of 170), and troops to the fortified region.

By then, however, most of the Austrian Crown Prince's assault units were already in position facing the enemy in the jump-off trenches. The Germans had set the date for the attack, codenamed *Gericht* (Judgment Day), for February 12.

But why Verdun?

After all, the area had proven its defensive capacity by withstanding German maneuvers in 1914. And with

crossed at its base by the Meuse River, an impediment that jeopardized both communication and supply lines to French troops on the east bank. On the German side, thick forest was available to screen assault preparations. The Germans would also be able to benefit from the dense and well-structured road and rail network behind their lines. Dynastic considerations came into play as well, as the German Fifth Army poised to attack at Verdun was under the command of Crown Prince Wilhelm, eldest son of the emperor and future heir to the Empire.

But beyond these military considerations, Falkenhayn

demand on manpower so that other fronts would not be dangerously exposed.

Falkenhayn believed that the massed power of his artillery would give him rapid control over this small, narrow, and partially isolated sector on the east bank of the Meuse and lead to the prompt fall of the city.

On the French side, confidence in permanent fortifications had been undermined in 1914, with the easy fall of the Belgian and French fortresses destroyed by German mortar shells. In August 1915, Joffre ordered strongholds such as Verdun

French supply truck.

January 1916: Fort Douaumont.

dismantled and transformed into "fortified regions."

Following this logic, the artillery in the forts, including flanking guns required for close range defense, were

Ground ploughed up by artillery.

improve the situation, but by February 1916 there was still only one road to Verdun, linking it to Bar-le-Duc. A railway line connected Verdun to the national rail

Shell holes used as trenches.

removed for use by field units. All that remained were the few guns in the gun turrets that were too heavy to be taken out. Manpower was affected as well, with the permanent garrisons eliminated and replaced by small territorial brigades of elderly reservists.

This failure to acknowledge the potential value of permanent fortifications is just one example of the blindness that had afflicted the military elite since the start of the war. What could account for such an obvious lack of common sense, when millions of men were holed up in makeshift trenches? Given the conditions they endured, concrete shelters of any kind should have seemed like a valuable asset to the defense system.

Since the beginning of 1915, the French headquarters were well aware of the sector's isolation. A few steps had been taken to

network, but it was regularly exposed to long-range enemy fire. That left the Meusien, a narrow regional line also running to Bar-le-Duc, but

German bombardier.

which was not adequate at the time for meeting the tremendous logistical needs of a major battle.

And yet all that was of little immediate concern to the men holding the sector. Early February had brought bitter cold, and they were

huddled deep in their dugouts, trying to escape the chill.

On the German side, 900 discreetly camouflaged artillery pieces, of which two-thirds were heavy guns, waited for the signal to open fire. The artillery would play a key role: the suddenness with which it would be discharged was intended to smash any attempt at resistance. It would brutally pulverize the front lines, and a

French aerial reconnaissance.

barrage of large caliber shells aimed at the communication trenches and the rear would isolate the survivors. But on February 12, the region was shrouded in a thick mist that prevented target observation. The attack was postponed by 24 hours.

Bad weather interfered again on February 13, and it went on to linger for days. On February 18, the assault troops, uncomfortably installed in their forward positions, were sent to the rear. The sky finally cleared on February 20 and, in very cold conditions, the men returned to the front lines.

In the meantime, French high command, receiving contradictory intelligence, again expressed strong doubts as to the imminence of an attack on Verdun.

On Monday, February 21, at 4:00 a.m., a single large marine shell blew up near the cathedral. Then, at 7:12 a.m. French time, 8:00 a.m. German time, brutal and intense gunfire erupted, progressively transforming into a bombardment of unprecedented violence. At 3:00 p.m. the shelling intensified, and at 4:45 p.m., with night falling, German infantry divisions came out of their trenches and began to advance along the east bank of the Meuse. The assault troops moved confidently toward the city, overtaking 5 miles of front.

The Battle of Verdun had begun. It would continue for 300 days and 300 nights.

On February 25, like a thunderbolt, the German army captured Fort Douaumont, providing imperial propagandists with a brilliant display of strength. The fall of Verdun seemed imminent.

For a dozen days, the Germans maintained pressure on French defenses, yet failed to breach the front.

Peugeot factory in Audincourt (Doubs).

French ordnance depot.

July 1916: Fort Douaumont.

Wounded French soldier being transported by the Germans.

Face Sud, côté S.E.

The south side of the defensive ditch of Fort Vaux.

Indeed, Joffre had finally responded, appointing General Philippe Pétain on February 25 to take up the defense of Verdun. Pétain had promptly organized positions on both sides of the Meuse and set out to correct the fatal deficiencies in the logistics lines.

On March 4, Falkenhayn was forced to admit the obvious: the surprise attack had been a failure. On March 6, he radically revised his objectives and expanded the offensive to the west bank of the Meuse. In light of the French determination to defend Verdun, Falkenhayn had adopted a new strategy: that of attrition. His vastly superior firepower, he believed, would rapidly cause massive casualties and deal a devastating blow to morale.

Attack, counterattack, air assault: the two nations were locked in a struggle to the death. The French had only one order: to hold the line.

Verdun.

Mort-homme, Côte 304, Avaucourt, and the Hayette ravine on the west bank and Douaumont, la Cail-lette,

Vaux, Fleury, and Thiaumont on the east became places the soldiers would forever associate with Hell. Ruins of villages, remnants of woodland, and vestiges of forts were taken, lost, and taken again, while the use of gas, flame throwers, and mines added to the soldiers' daily burden of misery.

Joffre, however, was incensed by the fact that the Germans had seized the initiative, and above all, he was irritated by Pétain's repeated demands for troops and munitions, which threatened to hamper his own offensive in the Somme. In late April, he distanced Pétain from the blood-soaked battlefield by appointing him to command the Center Army Group, and selected a rising star, General Robert Nivelle, to succeed him as commander at Verdun. But this did nothing to change the everyday reality of the French defenders, who remained under the fire of the dominant German artillery.

At the start of the battle, the Germans had controlled the skies and used aerial observation to ensure the accuracy of their artillery, but by April, French aircraft had regained air supremacy, braving danger to conduct regular and precise photo reconnaissance, artillery adjustment, and observation missions. The cumbersome and frail Farman and Caudron planes gradually received better protection from the increasingly energetic and audacious fighter escorts that challenged the enemy aircraft. Other flyers specialized in the destruction of German observation balloons. And still, slowly

but surely, the Germans nibbled away at the scorched, bloody ground, taking scraps of dirt and vestiges of forest, battered fortifications and ruined villages.

Adelphe Pousse, a country priest and regimental chaplain in Verdun, described his visit to the redoubt of Thiaumont as follows: "The Boches who captured it had been sealed off inside by our artillery. We walked doubled over through the human sludge, a mixture of water, mud, and corpses all around us. German boots with legs in them dangled from the tunnel walls—they belonged to the soldiers who had been crushed when the ceiling collapsed. We put mint-soaked cotton in our noses [...] What a horrible death for those men, for whom there had been no way out of the concrete."

Delousing during a bombardment.

July 1916: British heavy artillery on the Somme.

British stretcher-bearers.

for the fatherland to hold strong until the end and to crush the last attempts of an enemy in desperate circumstances." It was essential to head off a crisis of confidence. Left to spread among the soldiers, it might otherwise weaken discipline, undermine the authority of the commanders and bring the army to its downfall.

Among the Germans, the mood was somewhat different. After three months of ferocious battle, they had finally arrived at the line corresponding to the intermediate objectives they had set for themselves in February.

If they could get past this point, there should be nothing to prevent their triumphant entry into the battered town. And if Verdun were to fall, the road to Paris might open up.

But with the Allied offensive at the Somme taking shape, time was running out. On June 23, 19 German regiments advanced about four miles for an attack intended to bring the 120-day-old struggle to a decisive close. The situation quickly became alarming and critical for the French. The last line of defense overlooking Verdun was now within reach of the Kaiser's assault troops. But their "victorious advance" was checked once again.

For 10 days, the fighting raged with extreme violence. Both sides paid dearly for the possession of a few ruins, the charred stumps of trees, artillery-battered crests, and foul-smelling ravines poisoned by gas. For that abused strip of ground, churned up as if by a giant plough, the attacks continued. Some positions changed occupants several times on a given day. For the men, it was truly Hell, but for Pétain and Nivelle, things were looking up. They had just been notified that the Franco-British assault on the Somme was imminent. Joffre would finally be able

Meanwhile, Europe's socialist leaders met in Kienthal, Switzerland, where they issued an appeal for peace without annexation or indemnity and asked socialist ministers to withdraw from their cabinets and vote against any further war credits.

Horror after horror swept the shell-churned landscape of Verdun, which continued to roar, heave, and pitch. In February, the men had died of cold; now they died of thirst; tomorrow they would drown in mud.

No place was safe. On the morning of May 8, a powerful explosion rocked the German-occupied Fort Douaumont. With thick smoke filling the corridors, rescue efforts promptly got underway, but 650 soldiers and 25 officers were found dead. Bodies were piled in a corridor that was quickly sealed off, becoming a mass grave that remains to this day.

The battles continued. Falkenhayn, now well-in-formed about Allied preparations at the Somme, was extremely concerned about this new action on the western front. The only way to prevent or postpone the attack, he believed, was to continue the assaults on Verdun in order to wear down the relentless French army.

On June 2, German troops arrived at the ruined superstructure of Fort Vaux. The defenders resisted for five days, barricaded in corridors made unlivable by gas as they waited for reinforcements. On the morning of June 7, overcome by thirst, the garrison surrendered.

While the fall of Fort Vaux rattled an already war-weary population on the home front, commanders observed alarming signs of discouragement and loss of confidence in the field. Notified, Joffre responded on June 12 with a message to the soldiers at Verdun: "I call on you, by your courage, your sense of self-sacrifice, your passion and your love

First deployment of tanks by the British army.

113

to reclaim the initiative and impose his will on the enemy.

On July 1, 40 Allied divisions attacked the German positions.

The assault was intended to make the Crown Prince abandon his offensive, but the Germans held fast. As though attempting to change the course of fate, Falkenhayn (who would be replaced within days by the duo of Hindenburg and Ludendorff) decided to launch a last push. On July 11 at dawn, after exceptionally violent bombardment during which primarily chemical shells were used, the German regiments launched one more attack. That evening, Verdun seemed to be within reach at last. But on the morning of July 12, as 150 Germans made their way toward Fort Souville, a few hastily pulled together

Frenchmen—cooks, storehouse keepers and blue horizon soldiers hiding out in the fort—blocked the last German wave when it arrived, exhausted, just a few yards from the trenches.

Had they made it past the fort, the assailants would have seen the ruins of the unconquered city not far off. Instead, the force of will changed sides in that moment, in front of Verdun. The Crown Prince was ordered to go on the defensive and send his cannons and troops to the new theater at the Somme.

But Nivelle and his deputy, General Charles Mangin, did not wish to remain pinned down in uncomfortable and dangerous positions less than a mile from the last ridge line. Despite their limited means, they set out to push back the German lines.

July 28: Fort Sourville.

From July to mid-September, relentless and deadly fighting continued within a space of just a few square miles—an arena of truly inhuman misery and almost unimaginable deeds. Yet despite all the blood spilled, no significant

Rail-mounted heavy artillery.

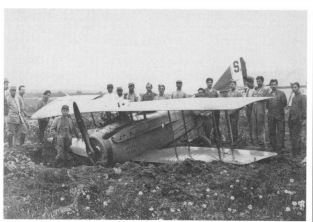
Downed French fighter plane.

reversals were achieved. A sort of equilibrium had settled in that seemed unshakable.

And the fighting continued. On September 4, it was the French troops' turn to suffer tragic disaster. The almost mile-long Tavannes railroad tunnel, used by the French as a command post, shelter, infirmary and storage facility, caught fire. More than 500 bodies were found in the ruins.

What was going on at the Somme in the meantime?

The violence and duration of the battles around Verdun had considerably diminished the resources available to Foch. Accordingly, the planned front of attack was reduced from 43 to 19 miles, with the lead role going to the British.

The battle had begun July 1, on both sides of the Somme River. British advances were quickly checked in many sectors. They suffered terrible losses, with 20,000 dead by the end of the first day. The French achieved encouraging results, but the partial failure of the British stopped Foch from pushing past the Somme as planned.

The great battle had not played out as Joffre had anticipated. Yet he pressed on, and fighting resumed on July 14. The second German defensive position was taken and progress was significant on the north bank, but limited on the south. Disagreement among the French generals delayed a new offensive. The assault was resumed on July 30 but became bogged down once again. Joffre responded with changes to the French command. Although still intent on launching another offensive across a large front with British support, he was unable to organize a coordinated assault.

And so the battle continued in the form of bloody piecemeal attacks. A new combined action planned for September 1 was postponed to September 10, then launched on September 4: Romania had just declared war on the Central Powers, and Joffre wanted to give the enemy a display of Allied cooperation. This third phase of the battle dragged on for 3 weeks. Heavy rain turned the battlefield into a terrifying quagmire, but it was during this period that the British first used their new tanks.

Despite the adverse weather conditions, Joffre was intent on persevering. To keep German reservists from coming to reinforce the front at the Somme, he ordered Nivelle to organize a new operation on the Verdun front. French troops recaptured Fort Douaumont on October 1, and Fort Vaux on November 1.

Joffre also insisted on continuing the struggle on the Somme throughout the month of October. In November, serious disagreements arose between the commanders of the two armies. New operations

commit more than 100 divisions—all its forces on the western front.

After firing some 24 million shells, the Germans had finally arrived within reach of Verdun, only to be driven almost all the way back to their February starting positions. Pétain, Nivelle, Mangin, and others reaped the honors, while Joffre, and now Foch as well, came under severe criticism.

How could the prickly commander of the French forces be discreetly reassigned? The situation was all the more delicate since he, in agreement with the other Allied military leaders, had already planned the military operations for the coming year.

Prime Minister Briand, a skilled operator, appointed Joffre as Commander in Chief of the French forces to avoid rousing public concern.

French 75 mm field gun, mounted for anti-aircraft defense.

ignation, which remained a secret. On December 27, a presidential decree promoted Joffre to Marshal of France. He was thus spared having to manage the profound war weariness that would seize the French troops in the months to come.

By the end of 1916, after 29 months of war, the front lines had changed little. From partial failures to incomplete achievements, the year had been a repeat of 1915, yet each side still held out hope for a decisive victory.

In other theaters, Romania, a major grain and petroleum producer, had been quickly defeated and was now under the joint control of the Central Powers. In Italy, no side had managed to gain the upper hand. On the Russian front, in accordance with Joffre's plan, a diversionary attack by

General Aleksei Brusilov had put brief pressure on the Austrians, but soon the eastern front was locked in stalemate once more, each side watching the other and awaiting its hour.

Grief, the pall of death, the anxiety of families, shortages, and the constant propagandizing had all begun to undermine the old certainties and prompt a gradual but profound shift in attitude. This was especially true for those directly exposed to the nightmarish conditions on the front.

Suffering, sacrifice, and death are not always acknowledged or fully appreciated by those who command and govern. The year 1917 would prove a profound and painful illustration of this.

Infirmary hall in the reconquered Fort Douaumont.

were attempted nonetheless, but the Battle of the Somme was in its final throes. Despite the intensity of the fighting and the quantities of men, guns and munitions deployed, no military solution had proven conclusive.

What had this hard-fought and costly attempt to dislodge the enemy accomplished? At best, the Battle of the Somme had limited and loosened the grip of the German effort in Verdun.

The Allied advance, which had reached as far as eight miles into occupied territory, had brutally worn down the enemy, trench by trench. Germany had needed to

The assignment required Joffre to abandon the command of the armies in the north and the east, making way for General Nivelle to succeed him. Nivelle's effective methods in the recapture of Fort Douaumont, his personality, and his efforts to please parliamentarians had all played in his favor.

At the same time, Briand granted the position of Minister of War to the authoritarian General Louis Lyautey, a military man unaccustomed to power sharing and criticism. Joffre, essentially a technical consultant to the government now, did not get along with him and submitted his res-

1916 by the Numbers

Franco-German Battle of Verdun. February 21 – December 15, 1916

French casualties: 163,000
French wounded: 195,000
German casualties: 143,000
German wounded: 180,000

Battle of the Somme. July 1 – November 15, 1916

British casualties: 206,000
British wounded: 213,000
French casualties: 66,000
French wounded: 130,000
German casualties: 270,000
German wounded: 135,000

1917

This would be a year of doubt and missed opportunities.

In December 1916, Germany offered to open peace negotiations with the Allies. Still militarily strong and buoyed by recent territorial gains in Europe, Berlin recognized the advantage it held. Should the Allies accept, Germany could expect satisfactory terms and the Kaiser would receive credit for putting an end to the bloodshed. Should they refuse, the Kaiser would be able to report to the nation and his armies that the Allies were intent on Germany's annihilation. This would give him grounds to continue the war, while "solemnly declining responsibility in the eyes of humanity and history."

The Allied leaders immediately indicated that they would not fall into the trap. Woodrow Wilson, President of the US, was approached to act as arbiter, and on December 16 he invited all belligerents to present a statement of their war aims. In early January, both sides replied that they would present their terms only at the negotiating table.

For his part, the American ambassador to Berlin believed that if the peace offer were refused, the Germans would have public opinion on their side and could resume total submarine warfare against Great Britain without fear of a hostile reaction from Washington.

The Chemin des Dames plateau.

In France, Robert Nivelle, who had replaced the disgraced Joffre as Commander-in-Chief of the army, now captured the nation's imagination. The "decisive battle" that would break the German lines was eagerly awaited, and people placed much hope in the persuasive new leader's promise of a swift and victorious end to the war. Even British army commander Douglas Haig was charmed. Nivelle laid out his tactics before Haig (sudden assault without long artillery preparation) and sold the British commander on his "surprise plan." Although several generals at the new French headquarters in Beauvais, including Pétain and French War Minister Hubert Lyautey, expressed concern about Nivelle's approach, a wave of enthusiasm swept through the halls of power in France.

Hindenburg and Ludendorf, meanwhile, were making plans to pull the German forces back to a new defensive line at Arras-Saint-Quentin-La Fère and had begun actively fortifying the area. Covering as many as 50 miles in some sectors, this major evacuation would let the Germans significantly shorten their front, save troops, and conduct a more effective defense. The generals' objective was to hold out until the terrorizing submarine campaign they advocated produced positive results.

Indeed, the two generals were looking for ways to hasten the end of the war. The Allied naval blockade had created severe shortages for Germany's civilians and, worse yet, for its wartime economy. Skillfully, they proceeded to silence differences of opinion in Berlin about the resumption of submarine warfare. These ranged from Chancellor Theobald von Bethmann-Holweg's concerns about the potentially devastating effects of unrestricted submarine warfare, to calls for its aggressive implementation by Admiral Alfred von Tirpitz, "father" and champion of Germany's submarine weapon, who assured that it would yield swift results.

Tirpitz was among those who believed that Britain would be compelled to seek peace within six months. In his memoirs, Ludendorff wrote: "Unrestricted submarine warfare was now the only means left to secure a victorious end to the war within a reasonable time. The loss of tonnage and the reduction of imports would create economic difficulties in England that would preclude the continuance of the war. I believed I could count on a decisive effect within twelve months, thus before America could enter the arena with her new formations."

The step was finally taken by decision of the Kaiser. On January 15, a German note informed the United States that unrestricted submarine warfare would resume on February 1. "All Allied and neutral vessels encountered in the North Sea, in the Atlantic down to Spain and in the territorial waters of Britain will risk being sunk without notice, with the exception of American transatlantic vessels recognized to be on a regular itinerary." A fleet of 128 submarines, including a number of ultra-modern vessels, was ready to give chase.

The Americans responded immediately by breaking off diplomatic relations with Germany. In France, Nivelle was preparing his brutal lightning assault. In so doing, he promoted the principle of bold attack even more vigorously than had Joffre's

circle. His plan of action was simple: organize a series of Franco-British attacks in the Somme—between Arras and Bapaume, and north of the Oise River—then break the German line in the Aisne sector. Preparatory artillery fire would last no longer than eight days. A 48-hour breakthrough assault would follow, after which forces would be pushed through the breaches.

Satisfied, Field Marshal Haig agreed to be under Nivelle's orders for the duration of the offensive, while the Russians and Italians committed to attacks on their respective fronts. Preparations got underway in the assault areas; the artillery took up their positions; orders were handed down. But then, abruptly, the Germans began their audacious withdrawal.

Nivelle initially refused to acknowledge the German evacuation and its implications: "It is highly unlikely that the enemy would abandon without a fight or without resisting to the utmost one of the main prizes he holds on our soil." When he finally accepted the fact of the withdrawal, he enthused: "The enemy is pulling back. The war of movement has begun." In fact, this development spelled catastrophe for the Nivelle plan. For one thing, the Germans had succeeded in pulling back unharassed and without losses to retrench in heavily fortified positions. As well, they had systematically devastated the areas they left behind: roads and communication

Kerensky addressing the Russian troops.

lines were destroyed, trees felled, wells poisoned, villages razed, manufacturing operations moved, and towns evacuated.

This vandalism received dramatic coverage by the Parisian press, which was always ready to disseminate the torrents of information and images released by the GQG (general headquarters). Though Nivelle's rudimentary plan of attack

was now thoroughly upset, he stubbornly refused to abandon it. As the two main fronts for his offensive (the Arras region for the British and the Chemin des Dames for the French) were mostly unaffected by the German withdrawal, he decided simply to adapt to the new situation by postponing operations. A number of senior officers expressed serious misgivings, including General Lyautey. Unaccustomed to the practices and sensitivities of parliament, however, Lyautey soon resigned from the post of Minister of War. Pétain considered the plan too reckless and warned of the risk of wearing down all reserves. Poincaré responded to these concerns by convening a meeting in Compiègne on April 6. There, Nivelle continued to insist on his strategy of breakthrough and exploitation. General Castelnau was circumspect when queried, while Generals Micheler and Franchet d'Espèrey expressed reservations. Pétain dismissed the plan straight out.

Outraged by the revolt of his subordinates, Nivelle threatened to resign. Poincaré stepped in to smooth things over: he assured Nivelle of the government's confidence in him, confirmed the political will for an attack, and granted the GQG sole authority in the matter. Nivelle was given freedom of action and preparations were resumed.

Meanwhile, in the United States, President Woodrow Wilson had summoned a special session of Congress on April 2 and, with its support, declared war against Germany. Two events had led the president to adopt this extreme measure: Germany's resumption of unrestricted submarine warfare two months earlier and the interception and decoding of a secret German telegram to the Mexican government. In the telegram, Berlin proposed a military alliance pledging to help Mexico reconquer lost territory in New Mexico, Texas, and Arizona. The

The first American troops arrive.

publication of the telegram tipped the scales, creating a strong current of popular sympathy for the Allied cause and leaving Wilson with no choice but to go to war.

It is true, too, that as Allied purchases in the United States increased, so did Allied borrowing. As such, American creditors came to have a strong economic stake in an Allied victory.

In the Allied camp, America's entry into the war brought welcome hope and relief. The agreement between Washington and the Allied governments, however, clearly specified that the United States would enter the war as an "associated power," not an "Allied power." Wilson was determined to reserve the role of arbiter for himself.

Developments in Russia, on the other hand, were anything but reassuring. In early March, new food restrictions prompted riots in the capital, Petrograd. Strikes paralyzed the economy, but when the Czar ordered his troops to restore order, the army sided with the insurgents. A faction of the rioters wanted the Duma (the Russian parliament) to take control of government. At the demand of the deputies, Czar Nicholas II abdicated on March 15. The parliamentarians, backed by

A French Saint-Chamond heavy tank.

a workers' council (or "soviet") and soldiers, formed a provisional government led by the lawyer Aleksander Kerensky. But while the provisional government promptly pledged to uphold all its alliances, the Petrograd Soviet called for negotiations with "the workers of enemy countries."

As such, events in Russia continued to worry the Allied powers. The fall of an autocratic and authoritarian regime and its replacement by a parliamentary democracy could only consolidate support worldwide for the ideals promoted by the Allies. But no government could ignore the specter of a war-weary army plagued by doubt or of troops refusing to fight.

A crushed shelter, Verdun.

While some dreamed of peace in order to foment revolution, others hoped the return of peace would prevent it. Switzerland emerged as a center for intrigues and maneuvering on both sides.

Lenin had been living there as a refugee, along with a number of revolutionary socialist friends. In March, Germany, wishing to further destabilize the Russian colossus, helped smuggle the exiled Lenin back to Russia in a diplomatically-sealed train. The Bolshevik Revolution was underway.

Meanwhile, Prince Sixtus of Bourbon-Parma, an officer in the Belgian army and brother to the Empress of Austria, queen of Hungary, was summoned via Switzerland to a series of discussions with Emperor Karl. But many in the Allied capitals considered the Austro-Hungarian monarchy to be hopelessly backward and obscurantist, and steps were taken to extinguish any prospect for a separate peace with Vienna.

In France, Nivelle continued to pore over his plans at the GQG in Beauvais, with little consideration for the political repercussions of America's entry into the war and events in Russia. April would be the month of victory. By putting pressure on the German front to the west in Artois and east of the Oise in the Aisne, the Nivelle offensive would force the Germans to make a deep retreat and liberate much of occupied France. This return to a war of movement, he believed, would benefit the Allied armies, which still had numbers on their side.

In preparation for the planned offensive, the British attacked on either side of Arras on Monday, April 9, the day after Easter. Though they captured Vimy Ridge, they failed to break the German defensive system.

would prompt the exodus of the German armies, weakened by the collapse of the central part of their defensive line. In practice, however, things looked different. The terrain was well-suited for defense: steep cliffs, deep underground quarries, concrete bunkers, and a well-organized battlefield awaited the assailants.

Nivelle had massed three armies for the assault, comprising all available French reserves. A total of 60 French divisions would take on 40 German divisions. It was the biggest concentration of artillery ever assembled. Some 5,400 cannons, including 2,000 heavy guns, were distributed along 37 miles, amounting to one cannon every 16 yards. For seven days, they hammered the German positions. Of course, the intense shelling eliminated any element of surprise. Worse yet, bad weather impeded air and ground observation, delaying the attack by 48 hours. Finally, on April 16, at 6 a.m., in cold, stormy weather, the troops came out of the trenches, only to face intact defenses, largely undam-

French infantry on the front line.

On April 12, the Northern Army Group under General Franchet d'Espèrey attacked near Saint-Quentin, but was quickly knocked out by enemy fire.

For Nivelle, however, these were merely secondary actions. The main effort would occur between Soissons and Reims, with the Chemin des Dames at its center. April 14 was set as the start date. In theory, the choice of this attack sector was sound. Breaking open the front at this location

aged networks of concertina wire, and precise machine gun fire in all sectors. It was as though the French had been expected. Indeed, for weeks already, leaks, rumors, and clues, including articles in the French papers, had alerted German command to the attack. Worse yet, during a minor penetration of the French lines a few days prior to the assault, the Germans had seized detailed operation orders for three army corps. They were amply fore-

French soldiers heading off on leave.

warned and had organized their defense accordingly.

Soon after 7 a.m., near Berry-au-Bac, French tanks were deployed for the first time. Eight groups of 16 Schneider tanks—slow and unwieldy behemoths—made their way toward the German lines. Advancing under enemy artillery fire, they arrived at the second lines at around 11 a.m. and crossed them in the early afternoon. But the accompanying troops did not follow, and the tanks found themselves under direct fire from German field artillery. By evening, the death toll was staggering. A total of 80 tanks had been lost, most with their crews. All told, more than 20,000 men died on that single day. Not one of Nivelle's objectives had been achieved.

Russian troops in France.

The attack was an unmitigated failure. For the troops, the great hope that had led up to this "last big push" gave way to bitter disillusionment. Nivelle could have put an end to the massacre, but instead he persisted, declaring the following day that victory was "ever more

certain." Fighting continued for three more days, spreading out toward the hills of Champagne. Advances were made, prisoners taken, and trenches captured, but at a terrible cost. Still Nivelle continued, disregarding the promise he had made at Compiègne to call off the offensive within 48 hours in the event of failure.

The government became concerned. Members of parliament criticized the conditions under which the attack had been conducted and its poor preparation. They berated the military health services for critical shortcomings, specifically in regard to the evacuation of the wounded. Arrangements had been made for only 10,000 casualties, far short of the 120,000 received. The operation was soon referred to as the "Charleroi" of the health services, in reference to the worst weeks of August 1914. The use of colonial troops came under scrutiny as well. The African tirailleurs (infantry), suffering extreme duress in the cold, rain, and snow, had been powerless in the face of enemy machine guns. Of the 10,000 tirailleurs deployed, 6,300 died.

Defeatism began to spread among troops and civilians alike. Nivelle was summoned and asked to explain himself, as he was preparing a new offensive for late April. In fact, in something like a repeat of past mistakes, he was transforming his "breakthrough battle" into a prolonged battle of exploitation. The facts were damning enough for the government to react. The

first step toward Nivelle's removal was taken with the appointment of Pétain as Chief of the General Staff. Was Pétain the eyes and ears of the government at the GQG?

But Nivelle was not done yet. In an attempt to shift the blame, he dismissed several of his subordinates. And between April 30 and May 5, he ordered new partial offensives on the Chemin des Dames and around Reims. The attacks resumed, futile and deadly, on targets that often proved unassailable.

Some generals remained determined to breach enemy lines, pointlessly putting men in harm's way. But others had the sense to object to the sacrifice of their troops and reported their concerns to the government. Furious, Nivelle challenged their claims, but his authority was greatly diminished.

American escort ships.

On May 15, the Council of Ministers finally replaced him with Pétain. It also put Foch back into a position of influence, appointing him as Chief of the General Staff and military advisor to the government.

The new generalissimo immediately announced an end to large-scale operations. It was a wise decision, but it dispelled any lingering hope for a quick end to the war.

The page seemed to have been turned on the Chemin des Dames. And yet in the weeks to come, this long country road, built in the 18th century for the daughters of Louis XV (hence the "Lady's Way"), would leave yet one more profound mark on the history of France.

For now, French military authorities had another problem to worry about. It involved the 20,000 Russian troops sent to France in 1916 at the request of General Joffre. Deployed east of the Chemin des Dames, they had suffered severe losses from the first day of the Nivelle offensive. Soldiers' committees had soon formed to represent the interests of the troops. At the end of June, the unruly Russian troops were moved to the remote La Courtine camp, in the Creuse region. But violent confrontations arose between Bolshevik partisans and loyalist troops, who sought refuge near Aubusson. In early September, the commander of the Russian troops in France presented an ultimatum to the rebels. When it was ignored, the loyalists, supported by French troops, opened fire.

The fighting lasted two days. Though the official count was eight dead, it is likely that many more lost their lives. Some sources suggest as many as a hundred or more victims, but strict censorship at the time meant that almost all traces of the events were destroyed. After October, Prime Minister Georges Clemenceau would give the Russian soldiers a choice: they could continue fighting on the side of France, become civilian workers, or join the disciplinary units stationed in North Africa. Had information about the situation reached the public, it would likely have compounded the intense disappointment that followed the failure of the Nivelle offensive.

Those dashed hopes coincided with an increase in labor unrest. As France's war industry grew, so did its unions, and they now took advantage of their growing numbers to take a more radical stance against the war. In big cities, large protest marches occurred daily.

Many women participated, following the example of the dressmakers' apprentices who had taken to the streets in spring. Cries of "Down with war!" often drowned out calls for higher wages. As he had done in 1914, Jean-Louis Malvy, the Minister of the Interior, took a conciliatory approach. He handled the press with consideration, negotiated with the unions, and avoided repressive action. Though his methods came under sharp criticism in political circles, they proved successful. Labor unrest gradually died down and was little more than a memory by early summer.

While the Socialists continued to uphold the *Union Sacrée* (the political truce between the left and right), some were beginning to call for *une paix blanche* ("a white peace"—a peace without victory on either side). When the government

British stretcher-bearers.

refused passports to a delegation preparing to attend an international socialist conference in Stockholm, the resulting controversy indicated considerable support for the opening of peace negotiations. Indeed, with all the sacrifices already made, some in France were asking: should more blood be shed for victory?

Meanwhile, cases of treason, corruption, espionage, and bribery made frequent headlines, often involv-

ing German attempts at demoralizing the French public by financially encouraging defeatism under the guise of pacifism within French media: These scandals included the secret purchase of the daily *Le Journal*—a transaction whose participants included Bolo Pacha, Henri Letellier, Gaston Duval, and Senator Charles Humbert—as well as another case involving surreptitious German influence on the left-wing paper *Le Bonnet rouge* and its editor, an anarchist who wrote under the pseudonym Almeyreda (an anagram of *y'a la merde*—"there is shit"). There was also the ravishing Mata Hari, an exotic dancer recruited by both German and French secret services, who had close ties to the civilian and military elite. One must distinguish the actions of this handful of misguided or corruptible individuals from the thoughtful and clear-sighted aims of the many well-intentioned peace-minded citizens who were urging an end to the destruction of European civilization.

Public opinion was split between support for a paix blanche, and commitment to fighting to the end to ensure that the nation's tremendous sacrifices had not been made in vain.

The failure of the Nivelle offensive had revealed the

shortcomings and mistakes of the high command, and the men on the front were losing confidence in their leaders. Military officials had noted alarming incidents of disobedience and desertion earlier, in the course of 1916. But that unrest had died down with the 1917 spring offensive and its promise of victory.

After May 5, 1917, however, as units were sent to relieve the front, a profound loss of morale becoming evident all along the Chemin des Dames. Men refused to go to the line, and they didn't hesitate to explain and justify their actions. Order was re-established again and again, but still the acts of "indiscipline" spread.

Two regiments were especially affected. At the 321st Infantry Regiment,

some 150 soldiers deserted upon being sent forward; a few hours later, 33 alleged instigators were referred to courts martial. The judgements took consideration of the men's fatigue and noted a lack of rigor on the part of the officers. No death sentences were handed down.

But for the 128th Infantry Regiment, things turned out differently. After having been deployed in futile attacks in Champagne, the regiment was relieved on May 15 and sent to the rear for some rest. On May 20, the men learned that they were to return to the line. The day was hot, wine flowed freely, and by evening, the men were extremely agitated. Two machine guns were turned on them before the mutineers finally marched to the front. Soon

British troops in Flanders.

French flamethrower.

after, seven of the rebels were tried and four were sentenced to death.

One, a teacher, managed to send a letter to the writer Anatole France.

"Condemned (...) after what was in reality a trial of beliefs, from my cell, I am fervently addressing the man and writer whose noble conscience and incomparable talent are universally celebrated (...) Sir, I place my trust in you." The government was alarmed, fearing that an execution could provoke further social unrest. The Minister of War, Paul Painlevé, appealed for clemency with Pétain and Poincaré.

Insubordination had already spread across the front, however, and acts of disobedience were becoming more frequent. Men sang the Internationale at the tops of their voices; camps were rife with sedition. Several regiments were getting organized to march on Paris.

German sentry.

A rumor spread through the units and became increasingly outlandish by the day: Southeast Asian soldiers, it was said, were massacring Parisian women. In fact, a street brawl had degenerated, a shot had been fired, and a woman had been fatally wounded. The exaggerated reports added to the bitterness of the soldiers. They had other grievances as well. They bristled at having to maintain training camp discipline in the chaos of the front. They wanted more and better food. They wanted a fair and regular leave system.

In some units, leave had been suspended for months because of the Nivelle offensive. Many officers, while condemning the acts of indiscipline, acknowledged the validity of the men's claims. The soldiers were not abandoning the trenches. Instead, they were simply demanding respect and protesting against ill-conceived offensive strategies. As committed "soldier citizens," they were refusing to be used as mere cannon fodder.

Soon mutiny spread across the entire front. Panic seized the government, which turned to Pétain to handle the crisis.

Given the urgency of the situation, Pétain wanted to bring back the severe courts martial of early 1914, but the government refused. However, the paths to appeal were partially suspended and, for one long month, Pétain had the provisional right to decide executions without having to submit clemency requests to the president.

This was also the time when the army's security service infiltrated the units with agent provocateurs. Their role was to stir up unrest, encourage agitators, and then report them.

Pétain moved swiftly to suppress unrest, but he also looked for solutions and introduced measures to alleviate the despair of his troops. Leave was re-established for a maximum number of men. Welcome services were organized in train stations. Better food was served and affordable military co-ops were created. The troops received new equipment and clothing, and

officers at all levels were instructed to take greater interest in their men. Talks were scheduled with the troops and Pétain took the time to personally tour the front lines.

Confidence was gradually restored. Little by little, the soldiers came to feel that their sacrifices and efforts were being recognized and their demands taken into account. Above all, it seemed that the days of futile attacks were over. By July, order was restored and healing could begin. Only after the fact did Hindenburg learn about the serious morale problems that had just shaken the French army.

The prudent Pétain proceeded to do what he had promised: "wait for the Americans, guns and tanks." In the following months, he launched only two significant but limited operations: one in Flanders with the British army in July, the other on the Verdun front in August. Well executed, they achieved their goals and gave the troops renewed confidence.

Of course, someone had to be found responsible for the disturbances that had shaken the army. Many commanders believed the troubles had begun on the home front. They blamed Parisians in general, and in particular pacifist intellectuals, union propaganda, the Minister of the Interior, and various newspapers.

And yet the root of the problem lay elsewhere: too much had been asked of the men. Between 30,000 and 40,000 soldiers had taken part in the collective indiscipline of 1917. Of these, 10% were tried. A total of 3,427 men were found guilty, 554 were sentenced to death, and some 50 were executed.

Still, the war did not end on the Chemin des Dames. Submarine warfare continued during these critical periods and threatened the wartime economies of both Britain and France. 800,000 tons were sent to the bottom of the sea in April, 1,174,000 in May, and 800,000 in June, before losses at last began to taper off.

The Allied deployment of thousands of patrols and escorted convoys and their

use of submarine grenades and sonar detection significantly curbed the operational effectiveness of the German submarines. This turnaround was a great disappointment to Berlin.

In June, under the command of General Pershing, the first Americans set foot on French soil, though much effort was still required to make an army of them.

Austrian mountain troops in the Dolomites.

The expeditionary corps was charged with creating the infrastructure to receive the troops: port facilities, reception and training camps, railroads, depots, and more. American industry was expected to contribute significant quantities of armaments and equipment, but to save time, it was up to France to equip the American troops with machine guns, cannons, aircraft, and, in 1918, tanks. In the meantime, Pétain entrusted a small sector of the front in Lorraine to this small and untrained army. America's first three fatalities occurred there, with the battle deaths of Thomas Enright, Merle Hay, and James Gresham.

By the end of 1917, fewer than 200,000 "Sammies" were in Europe. During this difficult time, it was up to the British army to remain active and hold fast against the Germans. It had reclaimed full autonomy and, in June, the British launched a series of attacks in various areas, including the Flanders front.

Camouflage: An artificial tree.

The Verdun front.

It was Haig's turn to initiate what he believed would be a decisive operation: an advance to the submarine base at Ostend, some 30 miles from the front. The plan was overly ambitious and the operation quickly came to a stall. Bad weather set in, and the battlefield became a terrifying sea of mud that engulfed cannons and swallowed up men. To add to the misery, the Germans introduced mustard gas, a new and especially insidious chemical warfare agent.

Once again, the two sides engaged in a costly and deadly battle of attrition. The air forces confronted each other. Sensationally, the French ace Georges Guynemer was hit and disappeared, presumably pulverized on the ground by shelling that devastated the sector. In early November, the capture of the village of Passchendaele marked the furthest point of advance for the Commonwealth forces in this offensive. In their strug-

gle over a small strip of land only 5 miles deep, the Allies had lost 300,000 men and the Germans, 260,000. For Britain and its empire, it was a tragedy equivalent to that of Verdun for the French.

In late October, soon after Pétain achieved a targeted victory on the Chemin des Dames, the site of the tragic April campaign, and shortly before the firing of the first cannon shot of the second Bolshevik revolution, another nasty surprise jolted the Allied powers.

An Austro-German offensive had just destroyed the Italian front at Caporetto. A lightning advance covering more than 55 miles had left the Italians "with their backs to the wall." Facing imminent disaster, they regrouped. The front was re-established along the Piave River with the help of a number of Allied divisions that were rushed to the site.

In France, at the most crucial moment of the war, with the army weakened,

the home front suffering, Britain bled dry, Italy at the edge of the abyss, Romania crushed, and a revolutionary Russia ready to stop fighting, Poincaré appointed the 74-year-old Clemenceau, a man he disliked, to serve as Prime Minister. An old political hand, referred to as "the Tiger" by those who had felt his claws, Clemenceau announced with all the authority of old age: "My aim is to be victorious ... I shall make no promises, I shall make war, that's all." He took charge of the country's fate in a near-dictatorial manner, refusing to compromise with those who wished to negotiate.

But already a new year was on the horizon, and all sides had reason for hope. The Central Powers had freed themselves of the Russian front, enabling them to transfer hundreds of thousands of men back to the western front. They had also gained access to Romania's abundant grain stores—an essential resource for the near future—and its petroleum installations. On the

Allied side, the American Expeditionary Force continued to grow, with a total of 42 divisions expected, and the French army appeared to have rebuilt its morale. The British had achieved important victories in Palestine, including the conquest of Jersualem. And Berlin was losing the submarine war. In both camps, a compromise peace was no longer an option: each was now aiming for a military victory.

On the front, in the chill of winter, one could still hear occasional snatches of the Chanson de Craonne, the anthem of the soldiers' despair in the summer of 1917: "After a week of leave / It's back to the trenches / We're so useful there / They'd get slammed without us / Farewelll to life, farewell to love / Farewell, all you women..."

1917 by the Numbers

French losses	**British losses**
April to October 1917:	**April to November 1917:**
Dead and missing: 167,000	Dead and missing: 250,000
Italian losses	**German losses 1917:**
August to November 1917:	Dead, missing, and prisoners
Dead, missing, and prisoners of war: 650,000	of war: 300,000

1918

The European war turned truly global in scope on December 7, 1917, when the US finally declared war on Austria-Hungary. Even so, the year's end was dominated by the reverberations of Russia's October Revolution.

In mid-November, Lenin had broadcast a radio message to the "peoples of the world," proposing universal peace "without indemnity and without annexation." Germany and Austria at once expressed interest in the offer. Berlin and Vienna were aware of developments in the Russian army, and concern about fraternization on the eastern front contributed to their willingness to seek a negotiated peace. First, it would cut off the stream of demoralizing—and potentially devastating—revolutionary Russian propaganda infiltrating their ranks. Second, it would free up troops for transfer, enabling the Central Powers to regain numerical superiority on the western front.

American field staff.

France and England answered Lenin's call for peace with silence. The Allies seemed taken aback by the Revolution, which they had welcomed in early 1917 but now viewed as a serious threat. The Russian military support they had expected had not materialized, and instead they were confronted by the victory of the Bolsheviks and their liberal and pacifist ideas. Moreover, peace on the Russian front effectively meant the end of the pact signed by the Allies in 1914 and was sure to result in a massive relocation of German and Austrian units to the French front. And what if developments in Russia stoked revolutionary and pacifist sentiment in France?

But there, Clemenceau's hard-line approach was already paying off. He had

March 1918: The German offensive.

reined in opponents and pacifists and put traitors on trial, all in the public eye. In doing so, he had gained a strong hold on the civilian population. And with Russia crumbling, the French government had turned its attention to building up America's military presence in Europe.

By this point, France had lost some 2,600,000 men—killed, missing, captured, or wounded.

On November 25, Pétain asked Colonel Edward Mandell House, President Wilson's emissary, to rapidly dispatch one million troops, with another million to follow. The request was all the more urgent given the news, received on November 21, that the Russian Council of People's Commissars intended to open negotiations with the Central Powers.

In fact, the Allies had been invited to take part in the talks as well. But they declined, on grounds that the Russian initiative violated the 1914 agreements. Unimpressed, the Bolsheviks submitted a request for an armistice to the supreme commanders of Germany and Austria on November 26. The cease-fire was almost immediate. A truce agreement was signed at Brest-Litovsk on December 15 and peace talks got underway on December 22. They were painfully laborious.

And then in January, the cunning Leon Trotsky, theorist and Commissioner of Foreign Affairs, arrived to head the Russian delegation. While the Central Powers wanted to focus on concrete issues, Trotsky stalled negotiations by countering with arguments for new rights of the people and a dictatorship of the proletariat—a diversionary tactic that unnerved and ultimately annoyed the German and Austrian statesmen. The Central Powers did, however, manage to negotiate and sign a separate peace treaty with the newly independent republic of Ukraine, to the satisfaction of Austrian Emperor Karl I. As Trotsky was well aware, this agreement threatened to undermine the Bolshevik revolution. He responded with characteristic aplomb: in early February, he announced that Russia was declaring an end to the state of war with Germany and preparing to order the complete demobilization of its troops.

Ludendorff, however, needed a treaty in the east that was consistent with a classic victory by arms. To this end, he ordered a resumption of hostilities.

He also wanted to isolate the Ukraine from revolutionary influences. Like many in Germany, he regarded Bolshevism as a threat to social order, detrimental not only to the interests of the Reich, but also to Germany's critical plans for the resumption of war on the western front.

On February 18, faced with a renewed German advance and determined to save the revolutionary regime at any cost, Lenin agreed to the peace treaty. Trotsky having refused to ratify it, Grigori Sokolnikov signed the agreement on Russia's behalf in Brest-Litovsk on March 2. After having lost the Ukraine, Russia now ceded the Russian part of Poland and the Baltic states to the Central Powers and recognized the independence of Finland. This territorial dismemberment was a loss Lenin was willing to take, provided the Revolution was saved.

The fall of the czarist regime meant the end of the Franco-Russian alliance. It also raised the prospect of substantial losses on the 16 billion gold francs loaned to Russia by French investors.

One of four all-black US regiments.

German assault troops.

The month of January was marked by another major event. In the US, President Woodrow Wilson presented to Congress fourteen points outlining the establishment of a league of nations after peace was restored. His advisor and personal emissary Colonel House was the driving force behind what was a bold diplomatic offensive, aimed at shaping the post-war world.

Tasked with coordinating the economic and military efforts of the Allied Powers and associated states, House had reported to Wilson his frustration at the lack of a diplomatic unit within the Allied constellation. Wilson responded with characteristic idealism. For months, he had witnessed repeated attempts to start talks, and he had openly declared that the German Kaiser remained an obstacle to peace. He now took the initiative to present the world with a detailed statement of America's war aims.

The Fourteen Points advocated the following: an end to secret negotiations; free trade; the absolute freedom of the seas; disarmament (with reciprocal guarantees); the settlement of colonial claims; Germany's evacuation of the territories it had invaded and of Alsace-Lorraine; the readjustment of the borders of Italy along lines of nationality; the evacuation of Romania, Serbia, and Montenegro; sovereignty for the Turkish parts of the Ottoman Empire with guarantees of security and autonomy for non-Turkish nationalities; the opening of the Dardanelles Straits to free

movement; the creation of an independent Polish state; and the formation of a general association of nations granting and assuring guarantees of political independence and territorial integrity to all nations, great and small.

Behind British lines.

Wilson hoped his initiative would pave the way for a fair and lasting peace. His high-minded proposals made no specific demands on behalf of the United States. They did, however, position Wilson as a key player in negotiations to come.

Wilson's plan satisfied some of the ambitions of the Arab and Slav peoples without dealing a stab in the back of the Austro-Hungarian and Turkish empires. Colonel House was already busy gathering information and documents for a future peace conference.

Colonel House soon became an ardent exponent of a league of nations tasked with

monitoring and settling international disputes. He was influenced in this by British diplomacy, which remained haunted by Germany's refusal to take part in crisis talks proposed in July 1914—a circumstance that British diplomats viewed as a direct cause for European nations entering the war. The concepts House now put forward drew on the reports of a British committee established in early 1918 to study ways of limiting the risk of war.

Though conducted secretly, the committee's deliberations were followed by House and would become the basis for the program Wilson presented at the first meetings of the Peace Conference held in December 1918. It was guided by a straightforward principle: give the world a legal code and judges that hold nations accountable to the same moral standards as individuals.

But back to January 1918. An exceptionally cold winter had fallen on Paris, with temperatures dipping below 7° F on January 5. Frozen waterways prevented supplies from reaching the city, and coal, already strictly rationed, was desperately lacking.

Food queues became increasingly common. Horses were slaughtered when hay ran short. "National bread" (adulterated to save on wheat flour) was limited to less than half a pound a day per adult, and the sale of meat was forbidden on Mondays and Tuesdays. Despite attempts at price control, the cost of items changed daily. While workers earned 1 to 2 francs

an hour, a quart of milk that cost 17 centimes in 1914 now sold for 2 francs. The cost of 2 pounds of bread had gone from 43 centimes to 2 francs, and 2 pounds of potatoes from 20 centimes to 12 francs, with only a three-day reserve in the city's storage depots.

Hard as conditions were in France, they were far worse in Germany. After three years of blockades, civilians were struggling to survive. Food was scarce in all households. Hindenburg and Ludendorff, now in de facto control of political decision making and responsible for the wartime economy, increased restrictions on the civilian population for the benefit of the troops. Turnips were the main staple. Meat and fat were hard to come by and strictly rationed (a few ounces per week). Sugar, coffee, and butter were replaced by substitutes. Wheat flour in bread was partly replaced by potato starch, corn husks, and even sawdust. By official ordnance, potato starch made up 10 percent of "K-Brot" (*Kriegsbrot*, or war bread) in 1914; by 1918, the percentage of flour substitute in "KK-Brot" had been increased to a thoroughly unpalatable 20 percent.

Even with ration tickets, civilians found food increasingly hard to come by. Every month saw a decrease in their allocated amounts, as Ludendorff cut costs and set aside stores to satisfy the needs of the lightning offensive he was preparing in great secrecy.

With their troops seriously depleted, the Allies dreaded such an attack. Pétain wanted to fight defensively while awaiting 1919, when he believed conditions would finally favor a military victory. The British essentially shared his views, though they called for an intensification of operations in the Middle East. Foch,

German gunners.

A French Saint-Chamond tank.

however, wanted the Allies to wage their decisive battle before year's end. These disagreements put even more pressure on the Allied Military Committee, which was attempting to define a form of unified command. Meanwhile, weapons and supplies crossed the Atlantic in quantities that fell far short of demand. And at the pace that troops were arriving, the Allies now realized that America could not possibly deliver on its commitment to send two million soldiers by December 1918.

The main problem was a shortage of ships. The situation did not improve until the crisis days of April, when Great Britain finally made all its ships available, and the United States commandeered a number of neutral vessels for war service.

In January, Pershing offered Pétain four American regiments, comprising mostly black soldiers overseen by white officers. It was a surprising gesture, given Pershing's insistence on establishing a fully independent and autonomous American army, fighting under its own flag.

Playing into his decision was the thorny issue of segregation and the use of black troops in combat. The ques-

British fighter plane.

tion divided both the public and those in command. Black community leaders had rallied behind the war, hoping to improve the situation of African Americans through the achievement of two short-term objectives: ensuring that blacks would serve as soldiers and not be relegated to tasks in the rear, even if they did so in segregated units; and seeing to the promotion of blacks as officers. This, they believed, could help change attitudes and counter prejudice in the United States.

As such, a token gesture was called for. But the military authorities were skeptical about the fighting ability of black soldiers. Some considered blacks physically well suited to combat but morally weak. Others argued that they lacked courage, aggressiveness, and determination under fire, but could be put to use driving vehicles or horse and mule teams.

The appointment of black officers met with even greater resistance. Opponents claimed that "blacks still naturally turn to whites for leadership" and that "a colored man does not readily and willingly obey a colored superior." "Colored foremen for colored troops is not logical. A colored man is utterly incapable of handling men of his race." (Arthur E. Barbeau and Florette Henri, *The Unknown Soldiers*. Philadelphia: Temple University Press, 1974.)

Such views were not uncommon. Many Americans feared that black veterans, aware of the rights they were acquiring through their sacrifices in the battlefield and trained in the handling of weapons, would return with demands for political free-

dom and desegregation—a radical change for America.

Given this sensitive context, Pershing decided to test the use of black regiments as fighting units in France, despite his publicly expressed reservations about the value of "negro" officers. The four black regiments assigned to the French army, outfitted with French weapons, equipment and helmets, went on to distinguish themselves with many honors.

Winter was advancing and the Allied military leaders had still not settled on a plan. In early February, the Supreme War Council of the Allied Military Committee met in Versailles. Foch's ideas were accepted, providing for a "general Allied reserve" under the direction of the Supreme War Council overseen by Foch. However, it proved impossible to put together such a reserve, and the Supreme War Council still lacked the powers to provide the necessary unity of command. Nonetheless, the usually reactive Clemenceau seemed willing to accept this flawed system. He trusted Pétain and, increasing the frequency of his extremely popular visits to the front, was confident that French soldiers had recovered their morale. But would this be enough?

On March 21, a massive barrage broke out on the front, from the town of Arras to the Oise River. Some sixty German divisions trained in new offensive tactics attacked the British positions and successfully forced a retreat. The Germans, advancing rapidly toward Amiens, were trying to drive a wedge between the British and French fronts. Would the two commanders, Haig and Pétain, be able to work together to hold the line?

In fact, their interests were too diverse. Rather than committing to the defense of Amiens, Haig focused on maintaining communication lines to ports on the English Channel. Pétain, concerned only with the protection of Paris, refused to spare even reinforcements to support the British.

Then came another surprise: on the morning of March 23, Parisians woke up to find the capital under German artillery fire. It was

soon determined that the barrage was coming from two cannons placed near Laon, some 75 miles away. On the opening day of this long-range bombardment campaign, 27 shells were fired, of which 18 hit the city, claiming the first victims. On March 29, during Good Friday mass, a shell fell on Saint Gervais church, killing 91 people. The shelling, however, did not shatter French morale, as had been intended: instead, it drew sharp condemnation from most Allied and neutral countries and only strengthened the resolve of Parisians. The last shells fell on August 9.

In all, German long-range guns killed 256 people in Paris and its suburbs and wounded 625. This was far fewer, however, than the deaths and injuries resulting from the aerial bombardment to which Paris had been subjected almost daily since the start of 1918.

The month of March also saw a new wave of labor unrest in the Paris region. The demonstrations appeared to be more concerned with politics than wage demands. The ripple effects of the Russian revolution were reaching the working class.

Paris bombarded by Gotha bombers.

By March 24, the military situation was so critical that Clemenceau worried the government might have to retreat to Bordeaux. Foch pressed for the establishment of unified command.

Haig, meanwhile, let it be known that without French support, he would begin pulling back toward Pas-de-Calais. Concern in London ran so high that the British War Cabinet sent a powerful senior member to France.

On March 25, Clemenceau, Foch, Pétain, and the British special envoy met in Compiègne. London needed French military support and appeared willing to swallow its pride: unified command under a French leader was proposed, and the British suggested that Foch be

Confidence had been restored and Pershing took the initiative of spontaneously offering his forces to the new leader for use as he saw fit.

The Germans did their utmost to widen the breach but met with stubborn resistance. On April 30, the German offensive ran out of steam and came to a stop. The Germans had advanced more than 43 miles and taken some 100,000 prisoners, but Ludendorff had failed to meet his strategic goal of "peace through vic-

Congestion behind American lines.

French troops pursuing the Germans.

appointed generalissimo of the Allied armies.

The next day, while shelling continued unabated, an emergency meeting was held in the town hall of Doullens. Asked for his views, Foch insisted on the importance of defending Amiens at all costs to prevent a break between the two armies, declaring: "We must not now retire a single inch." Tension was high at the meeting, and after numerous private discussions, a statement was adopted: "General Foch is appointed by the British and French governments to coordinate the actions of the Allied armies on the Western Front. To this end, he will come to an understanding with the Generals in Chief, who are requested to furnish him with all necessary information." Foch immediately left the meeting to turn his attention to the battlefield.

tory." Still, the Germans did not give up, and in April, May, June, and July, they continued to launch new attacks, attempting to "punch a hole" through the Allied lines.

On the other side, Foch was now the undisputed leader: appointed Commander-in-Chief of the Allied Armies on April 14, he went on to effectively limit or block German assaults. A major challenge arose on May 27, when German troops successfully stormed the Chemin des Dames. Over the next four days, the German army surged forward toward the Marne, as it had in 1914. Foch had been fooled: Despite Pétain's reservations, he had massed his armies in the north. Demands came quickly for the removal of several military leaders, including Pétain. Clemenceau had

to forcefully intervene to silence criticism and save the generalissimo. Foch sent in all the reinforcements he could spare. The American divisions were deployed and a bulwark was created. On June 4, the advance was halted.

The same situation played out repeatedly. The Allies would hurriedly round up reinforcements to stave off a German breakthrough, and the exhausted Germans would find themselves held in check yet again by a newly reestablished front.

The obvious weakness of his army compelled Ludendorff to keep up the initiative, in the hope that the fighting spirit of his troops could mask their fatigue for a little while longer. He knew that the morale of his combat units was suffering. Discipline was poor and looting and

desertions were increasingly common. German soldiers were beginning to feel the effects of their food rations, which were inadequate for the efforts asked of them.

Ludendorff decided to attack in a sector that he believed to be sparsely occupied: Champagne, on both sides of Reims. This final blow was intended to be the *Friedensturm*, or "peace offensive." On July 10, Foch received news of his adversary's intentions and directed all available reserves to Champagne. He also asked General Mangin to prepare a counteroffensive toward Soissons. For his part, Pétain deployed his forces according to his tactical doctrine of elastic defense-in-depth. It consisted in thinly holding the front line on which the enemy's attack would be concentrated, while awaiting the remaining German assault troops from strong rear positions that were out of reach of most enemy artillery support.

On the evening of July 14, everything was in place. When Crown Prince Wilhelm II arrived to monitor the battle on which the fate of the empire depended, the French artillery opened fire. The cannons could be heard all the way to the capital.

British soldiers in the underground quarries of Arras.

During the German retreat.

The German offensive was blocked on July 17. Allied aircraft, organized into bomber and fighter squadrons, had played a significant role in this achievement. Foch immediately began a counteroffensive. In the early morning hours of July 18, French infantry advanced from the Villers-Cotterêts woods, supported by 321 Renault tanks.

Caught off guard, the Germans fell back. But the Allies did not exploit this victory, incorrectly referred to as the "second battle of the Marne." Foch was preparing a new battle, and while he did not yet believe that it would be decisive, he knew that the tides were turning. On July 24, he convened Generals Pétain, Haig, and Pershing and presented his assessment of the situation: "The moment has come to abandon the general defensive attitude imposed on us until now by our numerical inferiority and to pass to the offensive."

His plan called for the implementation of five local operations before fall to secure the rail lines needed for the success of a general offensive. Foch wanted to keep pressure on the enemy but was not yet preparing the final campaign, which he expected would occur in 1919.

On August 7, Foch was made Marshal of France. The promotion ensured that his rank was at least equal to that of Douglas Haig, who had been granted a field marshal's baton several months earlier.

The next day, a combined French and British attack, supported by 456 tanks and moving under cover of artificial fog, advanced in the region of Montdidier. The German front was finally broken open: six divisions

were destroyed, and the material depletion and low morale of the army became fully apparent. In his journal, Ludendorff described August 8 as "a day of mourning" for the German forces. Another German general stated that "we are not being beaten by the genius of Foch, but simply by 'General Tank.'" Ludendorff, who had not believed in armored combat vehicles, discovered their extraordinary potential too late.

The Allied powers no longer made any attempt to spare Austria-Hungary in the hope of drawing it away from Berlin. Instead, they gave their full support to the various nationalities claiming independence, including the Czechs, Poles, Slovenes, and Croats. Indeed, the French government trained and equipped Polish and Czech refugee and volunteer divisions. It became clear that an Allied victory would mean the collapse of the Austro-Hungarian Empire.

Ludendorff, hamstrung by the poor morale of his soldiers, could see only one option: to retreat from the current fallback position toward the Rhine River, while maintaining a presence on French soil to give Berlin bargaining power in the negotiations to come.

On August 13, the Kaiser approved Ludendorff's plan, but stood firm on his refusal to participate in direct talks with the Allies. The Allied forces began to advance on August 20. By early September, the Germans had lost all the territory they had gained over the past four months. On September 13, they were forced further back by American divisions, organized into two autonomous

armies to pinch off the Saint-Mihiel Salient east of Verdun.

On September 26, the American army attacked once again—this time in Argonne, where Pershing believed he could prevent a German retreat by seizing Mézières and Sedan. But the inexperience of the general staff and poor logistics resulted in dangerous disorganization. The offensive achieved only limited results: the capture of the village and hill of Montfaucon. Elsewhere, the Allied advance was swift, and the Germans retreated in all sectors. Foch left the enemy no time to establish new positions, and Clemenceau let it be known that he would accept nothing less than Germany's unconditional surrender.

On September 28, Ludendorff, with Hindenburg's consent, nonetheless asked the German chancellor to propose an armistice. It was decided that a message would be sent to President Wilson to establish peace on the basis of the Fourteen Points, with the Kaiser allowing the implementation of parliamentary representation. On October 14, Wilson responded that the presence of Wilhelm II remained an obstacle to peace.

While the Allies sent out victorious communiqués with ever-increasing frequency and the French celebrated the gradual reconquest of their soil, major developments had been underway over the past month in the Balkans and the Ottoman Empire.

On September 15, French General Louis Franchet d'Espèrey, newly appointed commander of the Allied armies at Salonika, had gone on the offensive. In a coordinated assault, French, British, Serb, Italian, and Greek forces broke through the Bulgarian lines, and after a bold maneuver, the French cavalry entered Uskub. Faced with an upset liable to cost him his throne, Czar Ferdinand of Bulgaria broke with the Central Powers and ordered his generalissimo to request an armistice. The general conditions imposed by General Franchet were accepted.

These conditions included Bulgaria's evacuation of Greek and Serbian territories, the demobilization of its army, and the Allied occupation of various strategic points in Bulgaria. The armistice was signed on September 30. German Field Marshal August von Mackensen, who was in the region, considered it unlikely that the Allies could continue their advance north. But the Serbs, eager to return home, rushed forward, and the Austro-German troops were forced to withdraw from Serbia. On October 20, Belgrade was liberated. This major event sealed the fate of the German and Austro-Hungarian commanders, who had no forces available to prevent the Allied troops from crossing the Danube, invading Hungary, and entering Germany from its unprotected southeast front.

Defeat appeared inevitable. Franchet pressed on. He sent two French divisions toward

The Allied delegation led by Marshal Foch at Rethondes.

Romania in order to create a "French army of the Danube," charged with opening a new front behind the Hungarian positions. In support of this initiative, Romania remobilized and pushed back the German occupiers, commanded by Mackensen, who had no choice left but to return to Germany via Hungarian rail lines. In just a few weeks, the Army of the Orient had achieved the breakthrough that had been elusive on the western front. Its victory was devastating for Austria and set the stage for Germany's collapse.

On the Turkish front, the situation was equally desperate. Since September 19, British forces, supported by strong Arab contingents, had been battering the Ottoman

defenses. In early October, they annihilated the Turkish army in Palestine, commanded by German General Otto Liman von Sanders, while other British divisions moved toward Constantinople. London demanded a victory: "Turkey is a British affair. We have started her defeat and we are going to finish it." A hurried armistice was concluded on October 30 between the Turkish and the British. America, which had not declared war on Turkey, was not party to the agreement.

Only the Italian front had remained inactive, despite Foch's request for Italy to mount an attack in August. It was not until October 24 that Italy finally launched a counter-offensive.

The Allies capture one of the few German-made tanks.

By that time, Austria was already crumbling. Emperor Karl I had published a manifesto on October 17 inviting "his loyal people" to create a federation of autonomous states. The American response was scathing: autonomy for the nationalities was no longer enough. Nothing less than the dismemberment of the Austro-Hungarian Empire would now suffice. Meanwhile, revolution was brewing in Prague; Budapest declared Hungary a republic; the Polish seized Krakow; and regiments mutinied or fled. On November 3, Emperor Karl I, with no remaining authority and only scraps of territory left to his name, signed an armistice before fleeing to Hungary, which refused him residence. The ancient Habsburg dynasty had come to an end.

Now all that was left was Germany. Ludendorff had resigned on October 17. On November 5, Hindenburg decided to withdraw his armies to avoid their destruction, but he had no room left to maneuver. He asked the civilian powers to request and accept an immediate armistice. A message was sent to Foch, asking him to specify the protocol for the reception of a delegation of plenipotentiaries. Would the Allies want to pursue a complete military defeat of Germany through the destruction of its army on its own soil, or would they accept an armistice?

Foch, who was preparing a major offensive against Metz in Lorraine for November 14, could reasonably expect to deal a final blow to the remaining German forces. In Germany, sailors and arsenal workers in Kiel were rebelling; worker and soldier councils based on the Russian Soviet model had been formed in the big cities; Munich had declared a republic; and unrest was running high in Berlin. Germany was on the verge of revolution. The Allied governments agreed on the conditions of an armistice and Wilson informed Berlin on November 5 that Foch would be their sole counterpart in negotiations.

On November 7, Hindenburg asked for a truce "in the interest of humanity," submitted the names of Germany's plenipotentiaries and asked

where they should cross the lines. On November 8, the train carrying the German representatives pulled to a stop in an isolated clearing in the forest of Compiègne, and Foch put forth the conditions of the armistice to the German delegation. It had 72 hours to accept or refuse.

The conditions were not negotiable, and fighting continued as the Germans considered the offer. In Berlin, Chancellor Max de Bade was persuaded that revolution could only be prevented through the abdication of the Kaiser. But Wilhelm II refused. On November 9, as rioters protested, the chancellor took it upon himself to declare the abdication of the Kaiser and Imperial Prince. Minutes later, the Republic was announced.

The following day, the Kaiser sought refuge in Holland and the new government advised the plenipotentiaries to conclude the armistice before the deadline was up. It was signed on November 11, at 5 a.m., with hostilities to cease at 11 a.m. News of the agreement soon reached the public, and by 10 a.m., joyful crowds began spilling into the streets of the capital. It appeared that the nightmare had come to an end.

However, deadly fighting continued in the Ardennes, despite the conclusion of the armistice. At 10:50 a.m., a French liaison officer was on his way with orders for the 11 a.m. hot ration supplies. As he hurried to the village of Vrigne-Meuse, he was struck by a bullet and killed. He was the last soldier to die for France before the sounding of the cease-fire.

He was 40 years old. His name was August Trébuchon.

The Rethondes clearing, site of the armistice.

1919

The flame beneath the Arc de Triomphe.

The armistice had been signed, but did it mean peace?

November 11, 1918, marked the end of 1,561 days of anguish, hardship, and loss. Jubilation broke out in the streets, civilians danced and embraced. At the front, the soldiers were stunned by the sudden deafening silence. Only gradually would they come to realize their ordeal was over.

For a few hours, these responses—elation on the one hand, dazed relief on the other—allowed people to forget the losses, torment, and sacrifices they had endured. It was still too early to assess the full impact of the war or to imagine the possible consequences of the unfathomable carnage that had shaken the fledgling 20th century. But soon enough, the bells that had rung in 1914, calling nations to wage war in the name of self-defense, would be answered by those of 1919, tolling for 10 million lives lost.

In the days following the armistice, the German troops rapidly retreated to the borders of their shattered empire, taking along their weapons and equipment. There were those among the Allies who were convinced the war had been stopped prematurely. The final push, they believed, should have been completed through to the end, onto German soil; instead, Germany had been spared from inevitable and devastating military defeat through the signing of the armistice. But given the results achieved and despite

the legitimacy of some of those political and military claims, many were reluctant to impose further suffering and sacrifice on survivors who

had already given so much. Public opinion demanded an end to the nightmare. And so the Allies, though remaining ready to resume hostilities within 48 hours if necessary, began to make arrangements to quickly repatriate the American troops. In April 1919, more than one million doughboys sailed back home across the Atlantic.

The guns had barely cooled before the Allied governments began to worry about the potential "contagion" of the revolutionary princi-

The arrival of the French troops in Strasbourg.

ples promoted by Russia's Bolshevik regime. The troops of the Central Powers had been the first to be swayed by its propaganda. Attempts at Bolshevik insurrection were reported in Belgium and Portugal. The many prisoners of war returning from Germany spread the incendiary ideas they had encountered there, including the promotion of internationalism, reconciliation, and the "bolshevization" of states. Some in France worried that the red menace would replace the German one. Switzerland experienced large-scale popular uprisings and a general strike.

Defeated Germany, now in the hands of the socialist Council of Peoples' Commissars, which in turn

reported to the Executive Committee of Workers and Soldiers, was crumbling. Nonetheless, Germany was expected to honor the immediate terms and conditions of the armistice. The surrender to the Allies

of its planes, heavy artillery pieces, and machine guns was difficult enough, but the delivery of 5,000 trucks, 5,000 locomotives, and 150,000 railcars was perceived as a ruinous imposition. The Germans protested the requirement,

November 11, 1918: Paris.

November 11, 1918: New York.

American expeditionary force in Russia.

Friedrich Ebert, the German president, saluting returning German troops that had remained undefeated in Africa.

insisting that the handover of this quantity of material would disrupt the economy and prevent essential supplies from reaching the people. Germany did surrender its high seas fleet, however, and the event was spectacular. Escorted by all of the squadrons in the British navy, the fleet made its way to the bay of Scapa Flow, north of Scotland, where it

greeting troops returning from France: "I salute you who return unvanquished from the field of battle." His statement implied that the war had been lost, not by the German army, but by revolutionary movements on the home front, ignoring the fact that military defeat had been certain and imminent.

Confusion still reigned in Berlin. In the closing weeks of 1918, the city was seized by the Spartacus League, an extremist group led by Karl Liebknecht and Rosa Luxemburg and supported by workers, sailors, soldiers, and deserters. The Spartacists, who advocated a Russian-style radical revolution, clashed with the governing Social Democrats. Barricades were erected, street-fighting broke out,

the Democratic, Social Democratic, and Center parties. Its first tasks were to put down the revolution that was threatening German unity and, above all, to try to negotiate the conditions of the impending peace treaty with the Allies.

In Russia, the White Army was fighting the Bolshevik Red Army in a fratricidal civil war. The Allies grappled with how to respond. In contact with the White forces, the British were stationed in Arkhangelsk and Murmansk, the Americans and the Japanese were occupying Vladivostok, a Czech legion was in control of a portion of the Trans-Siberian railroad, and French troops had just arrived in Odessa. But the Allies did not fully trust the White Russian

ward spread of bolshevism. This containment strategy required the Allies to intervene in Hungary, Poland, Romania, and the Baltic countries. These, like many other nations in early 1919, had to contend with uprisings and powerful popular movements. Inflation, shortages, rationing, and unemployment mobilized workers and led to union actions and strikes of unprecedented size.

Meanwhile, the Allied leaders were meeting in Versailles and Paris. The actual negotiations played out among the "Big Four": Wilson, Clemenceau, Lloyd George, and, representing Italy, Vittorio Orlando. On behalf of the 27 coalition members (Russia, though invited, was absent), they discussed the settlement of the war and the peace conditions to be imposed on Germany.

As such, the "council of four" took it upon itself to decide the future of the world and its nations. The first of Wilson's Fourteen Points, namely the commitment to open diplomacy, was jettisoned from the start: although it was agreed that the treaty would be published in its entirety, it was also understood that discussions among the four would remain private (this despite the fact that transparency had been upheld as the key and indispensable condition for protecting the coming talks).

Fall 1918: Famine in Berlin.

was to be disarmed. Nobody could have guessed that this voyage would be the last for this modern navy, which had challenged Britain's command of the seas.

Even more surprising was an impressive military parade held in Berlin in March 1919 to welcome some one hundred survivors of Germany's undefeated protectorate force in Africa and their heroic leader, General Lettow Vorbeck. It echoed the spirit of the imprudent declaration made by German President Ebert in December 1918, upon

and retaliatory blows were exchanged between the revolutionaries and those upholding social order. In mid-January, anti-revolutionary ex-soldiers arrived in Berlin to put themselves under the command of the Social Democrats. Better-armed and more disciplined than the Spartacists, these Freikorps ("volunteer corps") units drowned the revolution in blood. Karl Liebknecht and Rosa Luxemburg were arrested and murdered. Order was restored in Berlin.

A new government was formed by a coalition of

leaders. Should military support be provided? It was a risky business, as the French High Command discovered when its war-weary forces mutinied in the Black Sea in April. Though the French squadron was pulled back to the Mediterranean in response to the protests, the sailors paid a heavy price for their actions, sentenced to imprisonment and hard labor in North Africa.

The Allies would eventually settle for establishing a cordon sanitaire around Russia—a buffer zone to protect Europe from the west-

In Northern France, the remains of a textile mill.

The governments themselves were excluded from the transactions, dealings, and concessions debated by the decision makers. The views of the four statesmen were often widely divergent, if not contradictory. Wilson wanted to establish a new world order and a universal and lasting peace. These would be upheld by a League of Nations, which would be created under the future peace treaty in order to give guiding principles to humanity and guaranteed rights to states. Clemenceau was not convinced. His aims were to establish Germany's sole responsibility for the war, stamp out "Prussian militarism," negotiate the neutralization or annexation of the left bank of the Rhine, and obtain reparations. "The Boche will pay," insisted Clemenceau, and the French were keen to find out how much, how, and when. The British wanted to maintain the balance of power in Europe, and thus demanded a treaty that would limit sources of friction among states and comply with principles of law and justice. They also, however, wanted to see the German navy dismantled.

Disarmed German submarines.

Italy's demands were based on untenable commitments set out in the 1915 Treaty of London—generous promises made by France, Russia, and England in return for Italy leaving the Triple Alliance to join the Allied Powers. However, the main articles of the treaty, which had specified various territorial gains for Italy, including tracts of Slav lands, were now in conflict with Wilson's higher principle of national self-determination.

As they worked out the most far-reaching peace settlement the world had ever seen, the lead players excluded the enemies from

Street barricade in Berlin.

negotiations and gave little place to the "small nations." Indeed, the other Allied delegates were mostly shut out from opportunities to debate and critique, and could do little more than listen and acquiesce.

The thorny issue of reparations quickly proved perplexing, and a permanent Commission on the Reparation of Damage was set up to reconcile the various and complex points of view. It had until May 1921 to assess, as comprehensively as possible, the total amount of reparations to be paid and damages to be compensated, though not a word would be said about debt. On May 7, the clauses of the treaty were officially communicated to the German delegation. Germany was given 15 days to submit written observations. But could it accept the treaty as it was?

When Germans read the articles and discovered the conditions imposed upon them, they responded with shock and indignation. The German cabinet considered the terms of the treaty excessive, unenforceable, and unacceptable. How could Germany accept a guilty verdict with no chance to defend itself and without access to the report of the Commission on the Responsibilities for the War? German parliamentarians

pointed out the obvious contradictions between Wilson's Fourteen Points (most of which Berlin had accepted before signing the armistice) and the Treaty provisions. After heated debate, they drafted counter-proposals for the Allied commission. With a few minor exceptions, all were rejected. Germans took to the streets to protest the humiliating *Diktat* ("decree"), as the imposed settlement quickly came to be called. The Allies responded by threatening to invade Germany. And to show their determination, they called on Foch to prepare his troops for a march on Berlin.

On June 22, after bitter deliberations, the Weimar Assembly agreed to ratify

the treaty, with two conditions: German parliamentarians demanded the removal of the article assigning responsibility for the war to Germany and its allies, and they refused to commit to the extradition of "war criminals." The Allies rejected these last-ditch demands.

Then Weimar received alarming news. Germany's entire high seas fleet, which had been interned in Scottish waters, had been scuttled by orders of its own admiral. In Berlin, French flags captured in 1870 had been burned by German officers of the Guard Regiment, in violation of the Treaty provision for their return to France. And in an ultimate threat, one hundred Allied

1919: Ruins of the city of Reims.

as crowds celebrated the glory of the French army. But some observers noted that if the staggering number of France's war dead could have been roused for a macabre procession, it would have taken 12 days and 12 nights for all to pass by. Those who had lost loved ones in the "War for Justice" were invited to gather at the foot of a monumental temporary cenotaph erected under the Arc de Triomphe, dedicated to those who had "died for their country."

It would be another year before the idea of a symbolic tomb for the unknown soldier would be taken up. For the moment, the unknown soldier was still a lost soul, wandering along the bloodied trenches that connected the North Sea to Switzerland. In 1920, the remains of an unidentified French combatant "of white race" were solemnly transported to their final resting place beneath the arch that dominates the Champs Elysées. An eternal flame, added to the site in 1923, was symbolically relit every evening by veterans associations in what would become a national ritual.

Peace meant long-awaited liberation for the hundreds of thousands of French conscripts aged 31 and younger who were still in active service; those between the ages of 32 and 48 had been discharged earlier and had already returned to their families. Coming home was rarely easy. Some of the men had been away since

divisions were poised to resume fighting within an hour of a potential refusal by Germany. In the opinion of General Wilhelm Groener, Commander-in-Chief of the German army, the Empire's few remaining forces would be unable to hold out for more than a couple of days. The Assembly had no choice but to yield. On June 28, the German delegation, headed by the Foreign Minister, acting "in the name of the German Empire and of each and every component State," signed what became known as the Treaty of Versailles. Only China, angered by the rejection of its own demands, refused to sign the treaty, which transferred to Japan the rights to Shantung acquired by Germany in 1898.

On all five continents, newspapers and newsreels presented images of the strange, historic, solemn, and memorable ceremony. The state of war had ended, but reconciliation was hardly at hand. The treaty still needed to be ratified by all governments concerned. Who would have thought that, a few weeks later, the American Senate would disavow President Wilson's framework for a new world order by refusing to ratify the document? In doing so, the American Senate blocked the United States from membership in the League of Nations and thus from playing a lead

July 14, 1919: Disabled veterans open the Bastille Day parade.

role in this organization, which soon proved incapable of fulfilling its mandate. A number of senators believed that the Treaty was too hard on Germany. Moreover, it was considered inconsistent with Washington's long-held isolationist position. Not until 1921 did the United States sign a separate treaty with Germany, the Treaty of Berlin.

On July 14, 1919, a grand ceremony marked the signing of the "Great Peace." Led by a thousand wounded veterans, a massive victory march of units from all Allied countries passed under the Arc de Triomphe. The impressive parade went on for hours

Mine shaft destroyed during the German retreat.

Physical rehabilitation for wounded veterans.

1913, and the transition to civilian life was a struggle for all. Their outlook had changed—often, it had hardened. Relationships had to be redefined and intimacy re-established. Many friends had disappeared. (Of the 940,000 young men called up for service from the classes of 1912, 1913, 1914 and 1915 alone, 308,000 never returned, having "died for France.")

The American hospital in Neuilly.

And how could the survivors even begin to speak of the suffering, the fear, and all the great and small miseries they had experienced during this terrible ordeal? Hospitals still cared for thousands of wounded veterans. Day after day, the war continued to claim victims as men succumbed to the effects of lung-searing gases, septicemia, gangrene, tuberculo-sis, or simply exhaustion—shell-shocked and shattered as they were. War widows dressed in black were everywhere, foretelling a decline in the birth rate that would penalize the country for decades to come. Although France had regained Alsace and Lorraine, the region now had 580,000 fewer inhabitants than in 1914. In schools, classes were taught by women, as more than half the mobilized teachers did not return.

There is no measuring all the human potential brutally cut off, all the talent lost before having achieved its promise, all the sparks of beauty and brilliance prematurely extinguished. Tomorrow's leaders had been lost—a group that would be unavailable to take action and fend off the dangers that would arise in the years to come. For now, responding to immediate needs, young veterans formed associations to secure their rights and obtain fair compensation for widows, orphans, the wounded, and the maimed.

Meanwhile, the negotiators were drafting the last paragraphs of four additional settlements completing the Treaty of Versailles. The Treaty of Saint-Germain, signed with the Republic of Austria, effectively dissolved the Austro-Hungarian Empire, to the benefit of various successor states. Under the agreement, the former empire lost 21 million subjects of a total population of 28 million, as well as 83,784 square miles of a territory that had previously covered 115,830 square miles. It was also cut off from direct access to the sea.

Hungary was treated just as roughly by the Treaty of Trianon, which destroyed its thousand-year-old geographic and historic integrity. Under the Treaty of Neuilly-sur-Seine, Bulgaria was forced to cede territory to its neighbors and enemies, the Romanians, Serbs, and Greeks. Today we know that these "subsidiary treaties," which divided Franz-Joseph's empire into eight successor states, would go on to become sources of significant irritation, tension, and conflict, creating incendiary situations not anticipated by those who drafted the agreements of 1919.

In 1920, the Turks, under the pressure of Allied artillery, signed the Treaty of Sèvres. This settlement, however, was obsolete before it was concluded, given developments under Mustapha Kemal and his National Party, which was openly opposed to the Allies. While the Allied commissions determined the mandates to be awarded to France (Syria and Cilicia), Italy (Adalia and the Caucasus), and Great Britain (Mesopotamia), and looked for a power willing to deal with Armenia, the Turks took up arms once again. The treaty, which had never been ratified, was considered null and void after the Turks won numerous battles. In 1923, a new text was signed in Lausanne, establishing the borders of modern Turkey.

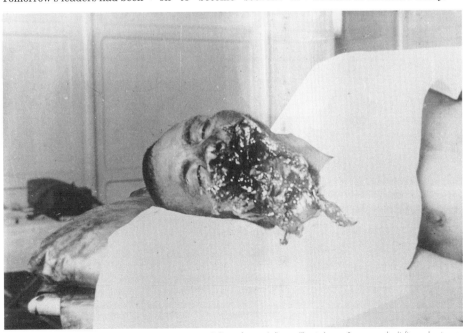

A "gueule cassée" — a "busted mug," or severely disfigured veteran.

June 28, 1919: Signing of the peace treaty in Versailles.

The cenotaph at the foot of the Arc de Triomphe.

What was the outcome of this half decade of war that marked the true beginning of the twentieth century? After four years, three months, and nine days of fervor and madness, would Europe be able to recover its pre-war supremacy? And what would the new Europe look like? Many people, especially the veterans, believed that the war they had just experienced should be *la der des ders*, the "war to end all wars." This notion was in line with the convictions that guided Wilson's plan for a League of Nations, mandated to maintain peace by preventing conflicts among states. Had the time finally come for an end to class and ethnic struggle?

But in the immediate post-war period, the grief, frustration, and opportunities created by the past four years had people craving relief, seeking out pleasure and embracing anti-establishment mores. Women had discovered their independence. The men who had returned from the war were forever marked by their experiences. The années folles—the "crazy years" of France's roaring twenties—were underway. But they couldn't dispel the burden of the slaughter that had set its mark on the 20th century. France had mobilized 8,410,000 men, including 540,000 colonial conscripts. It now mourned 1,400,000 dead, 3,600,000 wounded and 600,000 maimed, including 60,000 amputees. In 1914, it had been agreed

that the colonies would supply considerable contingents of "indigenous troops." By war's end, 70,000 colonial troops had died, including 35,000 North Africans. Their deaths were proof of the citizenship rights they had acquired, but it would be a while before frustrated demands for reform would cause the French empire to finally fall apart.

Of course, there was material damage and destruction to contend with as well. France's national assets had been reduced by some 30% and its most heavily industrialized regions devastated. A total of 1699 villages had been wiped off the map; another 2400 required substantial reconstruction. Some 320,000 homes had been destroyed and 313,000 partially damaged; 20,600 manufacturing facilities had been wrecked or pillaged; 5000 miles of railroad track and 32,000 miles of roadways needed rebuilding; 4900 bridges had been blown up. Vast expanses of land had been churned up by the shelling, including 5,253,000 acres of cropland, 1,062,000 of pasture land, 1,483,000 of woods, and 277,000 of built-up areas. The enemy had seized 840,000 cattle, 380,000 horses, 900,000 sheep, and 330,000 pigs. This was the demoralizing and nightmarish reality awaiting the hundreds of thousands of refugees who were gradually granted authorization to return to their homes. But many still believed that Germany

would pay for this massive destruction. None of the leaders who had single-mindedly sought victory over the past fifty-two months anticipated the upheavals to come, or the dramatic repercussions of the Treaty of Versailles. In December 1919, the journalist Henri Béraud and the writers Francis Carco and Roland Dorgelès granted an award for the worst book of the year. The winner was the Treaty of Versailles.

1914 – 1919: The Human Cost

The world saw tremendous losses during the war years, including 30 million deaths caused by the Spanish flu, a pandemic that struck in 1918 and burned itself out as 1919 came to a close. For the belligerent states, the further human costs of the war included:

74 million individuals mobilized	10 million maimed veterans
10 million war dead	9 million orphans
19 million war injured	5 million widows

ABOUT THE ARTIST

Jacques Tardi, who is in his fifth decade as one of the defining cartoonists of his generation, was born in Valence, France in 1946. Tardi broke into *Pilote* magazine with a series of short stories beginning in 1969, soon graduating to graphic novels. In 1976, he launched (for Editions Casterman) his early-20th-century serial *Adèle Blanc-Sec*, of which nine volumes have been released, most recently (after a decade-long hiatus) *Le Labyrinthe Infernal* in 2007. The unsmiling heroine's adventures were the subject of a film adaptation by director/producer Luc Besson in 2010.

Tardi's more than 30 graphic novels to date include a number of books about World War I (most recently the present volume) and a variety of detective and crime thrillers, of which five star Léo Malet's Paris-based private eye Nestor Burma. Tardi has won every major and minor European cartooning award, including the career-honoring Grand Prize of Angoulême in 1985.

From his studio in Paris, he continues to produce one remarkable graphic novel after another, most recently the two-volume *Moi René Tardi, prisonnier de guerre, Stalag II B*, about his father's experiences as a prisoner of war during World War II.

ABOUT THE WRITER

A long-time collector of objects and photographs from World War I, Jean-Pierre Verney contacted Jacques Tardi during the 1980s serialization of his first major work on the subject, *It Was the War of the Trenches*, in *[À Suivre]* magazine, to correct some minor errors. An initially reluctant Tardi soon embraced Verney's counsel and contributions, and has since then relied extensively on both his knowledge and his collection for his subsequent World War I-related books.

In 2005, Verney's entire collection was purchased by the state: the resultant museum, the *Musée de la Grande Guerre du Pays de Meaux*, opened in November, 2011 in a ceremony presided over by then-President Nicolas Sarkozy. Its website can be accessed here: http://www.museedelagrandeguerre.eu/en. Verney also served as a technical consultant on the movie *A Very Long Engagement*, directed by Jean-Pierre Jeunet.

ABOUT THIS BOOK

Created a decade after the completion of *It Was the War of the Trenches, Goddamn This War! (Putain de Guerre!)* was initially serialized in six newspaper-format pamphlets, and then released in two volumes. *Goddamn This War!* is the ninth volume of Tardi's work to be released in English by Fantagraphics Books.